A Year Without Autumn

Liz Kessler

Orion
Children's Books

ORION CHILDREN'S BOOKS

First published in Great Britain in 2011 by Orion Children's Books
This edition published in 2017 by Hodder and Stoughton

15

A CIP catalogue record for this book
is available from the British Library.

ISBN 978 1 4440 0321 5

Printed and bound in Great Britain
by Clays Ltd, Elcograf S.p.A.

The paper and board used in this book are
made from wood from responsible sources.

Orion Children's Books
An imprint of
Hachette Children's Group
Part of Hodder and Stoughton
Carmelite House
50 Victoria Embankment
London EC4Y 0DZ

An Hachette UK Company
www.hachette.co.uk

www.hachettechildrens.co.uk

*This book is dedicated to Judith Elliott,
to say thank you for eight years of sharing
your wisdom, patience, ideas, kindness and
inspiration. It's been a privilege to work
with you and to learn from the best.*

'And in today already walks tomorrow.'

– Friedrich von Schiller

1

'Stop the car!'

'What?' Dad swivels round in his seat. The car jerks into a swerve.

'Good grief, Tom!' Mum squeals, gripping her arm-rest as she pulls a wad of tissues out of her bag.

'Stop the car!' I repeat. It's going to be too late in a minute. I grab the tissues from Mum and shove them over Craig's mouth.

Dad pulls over just in time and Craig lurches out of his seat, runs to the gravelly path by the side of the road and doubles over.

The car stinks of sick for the rest of the journey.

I sniff pointedly. 'Mmm, get a load of that fresh country air.'

Craig pinches me. 'I didn't even do it in the car, Jenni,' he mumbles under his breath as I open my window and stick my head out.

Welcome to the Green family holiday. Green by name, green by nature, if my little brother's face is anything to go by. Mum's isn't much better, either. But then she is eight months pregnant so she's got an excuse for feeling a bit delicate – especially when Dad's behind the wheel.

Honestly, I could predict this journey with my eyes closed. It's the same every year. An hour of Dad driving too fast round the bendy 'A' roads, during which Mum will ask him to slow down at least ten times and Craig will puke at least once, followed by three hours of crawling up the motorway with ten trillion other families who have suddenly realised there's only one more week of the summer holidays.

Then we'll arrive at our timeshare apartment which will look exactly the same as it does every year, and exactly the same as all the other apartments at River-side Village: big open plan living room and kitchen, both beige and cream, both spotlessly clean and tidy. No dirty stains on the brown leather sofa. No finger marks on the telly. Microwave, sandwich maker, washing up rack, fruit bowl – everything labelled and ticked off in the Guest File, and sitting neatly in its place. In the place it's been when we've come into the apartment on the last Saturday of August every year, ever since I can remember.

But we like it like that. That's the thing about my family. We like order; we like to be in the right place at the right time. We don't like surprises or change very much. I guess that's why we have a timeshare apartment; so we know exactly what to expect. Same thing, every year. I could even tell you which leaves will have started to turn red. It's always the same ones. Every year.

'Perfect,' Dad says with a satisfied nod as he pulls into the drive. 'Fourteen hundred hours.' Which is two o' clock for normal people. The exact time we're allowed into the apartment.

'Bang on time,' Mum says with a smile. 'Well done, darling.'

That's what they like to be, my mum and dad. Bang on time.

There's a strange comfort as we unpack the car and settle in. It's a bit like when winter comes and you dig out those big fluffy jumpers that you haven't thought about all year but you suddenly remember you love, and you're glad you've got the chance to wear them again.

There's a huge telly in the middle of the room that swivels all the way round, so you can watch it from anywhere. And there's a bed that folds out from the wall, which you'd never notice unless you knew it was there; it's like something you'd get in a James Bond film. Not that we ever use it – but just knowing it's there feels a bit exotic and mysterious. And there's always a tray of sweets on the table to welcome you. I let Craig dive for the sweets while I take my bags to the room we share, so I can get the best bed by the window.

I hate sharing with Craig. For one thing, he snores

and grunts all night, and I have to creep around in the dark when I come to bed so I don't wake him up. And then he babbles about all sorts of nonsense in the morning, telling me about his dreams of monsters made from jelly. And for another—

'Budge up, sis.'

Right on cue, the little monster barges in, plonks his rucksack on the other bed and starts pulling out its contents.

Approximately thirty seconds later, his bed and half the floor space are completely buried under a pile of clothes, a small mountain of Lego pieces, five packets of sweets, three pairs of dirty trainers, and about fifty model cars, buses and tractors.

'Done!' he says, shoving his rucksack under the bed and folding his arms.

'Done?' I say. 'Done what?'

'Unpacked,' he says simply. He grabs a handful of Lego bricks and heads for the door.

Once he's gone, I stare at the bombsite he's left behind and take a deep breath.

Like I said, I *hate* sharing with Craig.

I guess I'm quite mature for my age. Everyone says so. 'Twelve going on twenty,' my dad says. I'm the oldest in my year at school, and the oldest child in the family. Sometimes it gets a bit annoying always having to be the older, sensible one – but I suppose that's just how I am.

There's a 'thump thump thump' along the corridor and Craig appears in the room again.

He grabs another handful of Lego bricks, then rifles through various jeans pockets till he finds a bag of sweets left behind goodness knows how many eons ago. He peels a lemon bonbon from the bag and hands it to me. While I'm looking at it and wondering exactly where it's been, he unwraps a chewy lollipop for himself.

'What goes "Ha ha bonk"?' he reads from the wrapper.

'I don't know,' I say.

'A man laughing his head off.'

There's a pause as he lets the joke digest. A second later, he falls forward on his bed and guffaws in his inimitable half choke, half hyena giggle that I can't help smiling at, despite my irritation.

That's the thing with Craig. He's the only person who really winds me up, the only one who can make me want to scream with frustration, but then sometimes he can make me laugh so much I cry. The only other person who can do that is Autumn. She's the funniest person in the world, and the brightest and smartest and all-round fabulousest! And she's my best friend!

Dad pokes his head round the door. 'Fancy a wander, Jenni bear?'

'Yeah, why not?' I reply, wincing slightly at the pet name he's had for me since I was about three. I haven't got the heart to ask him not to use it; he'd be all hurt, and that would be even worse than being called baby names.

I put the last of my clothes into a drawer and shove my rucksack into the wardrobe. On the way downstairs, I pull my hair into a pony tail with a scrunchy. It's driving me mad at the moment. It falls all over my face in loopy ringlets if I don't tie it back.

'Depriving us of your lovely curly locks again?' Dad says with a wink as I join him and Mum in the living room. If they had their way, I'd let it grow down to my knees, but I'm determined to get it cut, once I can persuade them it's not the end of the world. They're scared it'll be the start of a slippery slope. I've tried to explain that a change of hairstyle doesn't automatically lead to two-inch thick make-up, multiple piercings and a tattooed neck, but they're not convinced yet. So I just smile, and discreetly pull my scrunchy a little bit tighter.

Craig is sprawled out on the living room floor, making an incredibly complex-looking robot out of Lego. Mum's propped up on the sofa with a magazine and a cup of tea.

'Take it easy,' Dad says, reaching over to kiss her forehead and pat her eight months pregnant tummy.

He ruffles Craig's hair on his way across the room. 'See you later, kid,' he says. Craig doesn't look up. He's concentrating too hard on the robot, his tongue poking tightly out of the side of his mouth.

Dad takes my hand while we walk along the gravelly path. I stop myself from pulling away and reminding him that I'm not five years old. Instead, I let him hold it for a minute, and then pretend I have to scratch my nose so I can let go.

We walk past the second block of the complex. Together with ours, it's the modern part of Riverside Village. These two buildings were only added on about ten years ago. The other two buildings have been here for nearly a hundred years. One of them, the reception block, is ahead of us, an elongated cottage with a thatched roof and bushy green ivy all over the walls. Autumn's block is almost opposite reception, and is the grandest of the lot. Autumn's family have one of the posh apartments on the first floor. They were updated at the same time as our block was added, and they all have huge bedrooms, massive terraces and Jacuzzis in all three bedrooms!

We're just walking between the two buildings when the sound of a loud horn behind us nearly makes me jump out of my skin. I spin round to see a red Porsche roaring towards us.

'Autumn!' I run over to meet them as they pull up in the car park.

Autumn waves madly from the tiny back seat where she and her little brother Mikey are both scrunched up with their knees practically behind their ears, suitcases on their laps and most of the window space taken up with bags.

Autumn's dad is an artist, and her mum is the manager at the gallery where he sells his work. He bought the car as a present for himself when they sold one of his paintings for a whopping amount. He wouldn't tell us how much it went for, but Mrs Leonard said it could have bought them a new kitchen. So that was what he bought as *her* present when they sold the next painting!

Autumn's parents are totally fab. It's always crazy round at their house. There are always loads of people coming round to visit and they're always throwing dinner parties and having mad conversations where everyone talks at once, and no one ever tells Autumn or Mikey it's time for bed, and she gets to do things like bake bread and paint murals on the walls. We even helped her dad make cocktails once, for a party they were throwing. That was so cool. Bright red and green drinks, and we served them to all their artist friends in glasses that we frosted with pink sugar.

Their house always smells of incense that they've brought back from some exotic holiday or other. I feel like I'm on holiday myself when I'm round there. It's *so* different from our house. Nothing changes from one day to the next at home, and nothing's ever a mess. Although I kind of like that, too. At least you know where you are.

I guess Autumn's folks must like having at least one week of the year where life is a bit more ordered. I can't think of any other reason why they'd come to Riverside Village – except to see us of course! Although I don't understand that one either! Sometimes I wonder why Autumn would want me as her best friend. I'm nowhere near as interesting as she is. Whenever I tell her that, she just laughs and says I'm being stupid and we're best friends forever. And even though I still don't get why she chose me, I know it's true. She'd never lie to me.

Mrs Leonard peels herself out of the car and smiles at me. 'Hello Jenni love,' she says. 'How's Mum?' She comes over and kisses me on both cheeks.

'She's fine,' I say, blushing at the exotic greeting. 'She's back at the apartment with Craig.'

'Putting her feet up for once,' Dad adds.

Autumn's mum and my mum are best friends too. They met at about the same time as us. While Autumn and I were splatting paint at each other and sharing books way back in Year One, our mums were swapping recipes and gossiping about our teachers outside in the playground. Dad and Mr Leonard have become friends as well.

Autumn and Mikey tumble out of the car. Mikey doesn't look up from the electronic game he's more or less attached to. Autumn runs straight round the car to me, red hair flying.

'Jenni!' she yells, and we fling our arms round each other and jump up and down on the spot.

Mr Leonard gets out of the car and gently closes the door behind him. 'Watch the car, girls,' he says, warding us away from his pride and joy. He reaches out to shake Dad's hand and nods across at us. 'Wouldn't think this pair only saw each other yesterday, would you?' he says with a smile.

'*Yesterday?*' Dad replies in mock horror. 'But that's a whole DAY ago. That's practically a lifetime!'

'Ha ha, very funny,' Autumn retorts. 'For your information, there's a *million* things Jenni and I need to share since yesterday. Aren't there, Jenni?'

I giggle and grin at Autumn. 'At *least* a million,' I say. 'Maybe even a million and a half.'

'Right, well they'll all have to wait, because I need a hand with these,' Mr Leonard says as he pulls the last of their cases out of the car.

I stare at the pile of matching designer cases next to the Porsche.

'How on earth did you get it all in?' I ask.

Autumn beams at me. 'It's the Tardis – didn't you know?' she says, her eyes glinting with mischievous delight. She spins round and waves her arms around her, making creepy time-machine noises.

Mikey looks up for the first time. 'The Tardis?' he says. 'Where?'

Mrs Leonard strokes his cheek. 'Your sister's joking, sweetheart,' she says. 'It's not a Tardis at all. It's a Porsche. Otherwise known as a middle-aged man's mid-life crisis.'

Mikey screws his nose up and looks at his mum. 'What's that?' he says. Autumn smiles affectionately at her brother. 'Just boring grown-up stuff, nothing for us to worry about, kid,' she says, ruffling his hair.

Mikey shrugs off the ruffle and goes back to his game.

'Kid brothers,' she says with a dramatic sigh. 'Don't you just love them?'

She's joking but I know she means it really. Mikey brings out Autumn's love and protectiveness like no one else can. I guess he's to her what Craig is to me. We love them to death – but we wouldn't tell them in a million years!

Mikey's eight. Two years older than Craig, so they're not best friends or anything, but they hang out a bit when we're here, which makes Craig feel very grown up. Although 'hanging out' might be a slight exaggeration. It's generally a case of Mikey sitting around playing on his latest game and Craig being given the privilege of watching. Still, it works for them.

'Right, come on,' Dad says, reaching for my hand and pulling me away. 'Let's leave them to it. I'm sure the million and a half things can last till later. See you guys at Reception for the welcome meeting?'

The welcome meeting is when the Riverside Village people tell us what activities are going to be on during the week. There's a little cinema inside the reception block where they show a different film every night, and there are always loads of things going on each day, trips out and stuff. Everything from bird watching trips to hot air balloon rides.

'Absolutely!' Autumn's parents say in unison.

Autumn jumps to attention and salutes. 'Aye, aye, cap'n, see you there,' she says and blows me a kiss in the air as she runs off to help her parents with the bags.

I can't help wondering what crazy activity Autumn will rope me into at this year's welcome meeting. She always tries to drag me off on some zany trip – and I usually end up going. I can't imagine saying no to Autumn over anything. I think it's got something to do with the gleam in her eyes, and the laughter on her face. You always know that if she suggests something, it'll probably be half mad, half bad but 100% better than anything else – as long as you do it with her. She could make bricklaying seem exciting! Don't ask me how; she just could.

If it wasn't for Autumn, I'd avoid any of the adventure trips. I prefer to visit museums with my mum. I know that sounds boring, but I don't think it is. Museums open my mind and make my imagination run away with itself. All those old objects and strange artefacts make me think about all the people who existed and used them before me, and wonder what their lives were like.

And Dad usually drags us out on at least two mammoth walks while we're here. Walking is Dad's big thing. That and writing. He's – well, he'd say he's a writer but that's just because he's been going to this creative writing class and the teacher told them they all have to call themselves writers. She says that's the first step. Personally, I'd have thought the first step would be putting pen to paper, but that's just my opinion.

He's really a maths teacher. Deputy head of maths at the same school that I go to! How embarrassing is *that*? Actually, Year Seven wasn't too bad. I wasn't in his set, and as long as I never get him as my form tutor, I don't mind *too* much. Mum's a counsellor at the university in the next town. She doesn't talk much about her work because she has to virtually sign the official secrets act every time someone speaks to her.

Dad and I walk along beside the river. A great big swan and two fluffy brown cygnets are paddling in the water, swept along sideways by the rush of the current. It's gushing past faster than I've ever seen it.

'River's full,' Dad says swinging my arm as we walk.

'It's in a hurry,' I say.

Dad stands back from me and stares for a second. 'That's good,' he says. 'I like it.' Then he gets out his notebook and scribbles down what I said. You have to be careful around Dad. When he's in one of his 'creative' moods, pretty much anything you say could get jotted down and saved up for the day he writes his bestselling novel.

I say novel. What it really is, if we're honest, is a notebook that he's had for years, stuffed with scraps of paper and torn cigarette packet lids and napkins where he's scribbled tiny half ideas and the odd line of poetry.

He says that's the mark of a real novelist, the fact that he carries this notebook around. I've tried telling him the mark of a real novelist is a real novel, but he just closes his eyes and smiles to himself in that way that means he knows the real truths about life and I'll understand when I'm older.

I write a bit too, but only in my diary. I've never shown it to anyone. I'd die before doing that, although

I sometimes read bits out to Autumn. She always points out hidden meanings in what I've written, picking up on every little thing to tell me something about myself that I hadn't noticed when I wrote it. She makes me sound much more interesting than I really am!

Autumn doesn't keep a diary. She wouldn't have the patience. Everything she does has to involve moving about, preferably outside, even when it's raining. She can't bear to sit still. She goes rock climbing with her dad and goes to a weird dance class that a friend of her mum's runs. She's tried to get me to go to it with her but I can't dance. I've tried it but I just freeze up. I turn so stiff I feel as though I'm wearing a suit of armour.

You might be wondering what exactly we have in common. I do too, sometimes. But it's as if we're two different halves of one whole or something. I can talk to her about absolutely anything, and she's the same with me. We never get bored of each other's lives. We have to share everything – every last detail.

Dad and I stand watching the water foam and fight as it rushes to get under the bridge. A couple of lads in trainers and shorts climb on to the wall and we watch them prepare to jump into the swirling water.

'I tell you,' Dad says, shaking his head as the first boy splashes loudly into the water, 'if either of you kids ever thinks about doing that—'

'Don't worry, Dad,' I laugh. 'I wouldn't dream of it!' We have the same conversation every year. How he even thinks I might consider it, I don't know.

'GERONIMO!' Another splash as the next boy pounds into the river.

I shudder as we move on, down to the weir. One year, we'd had a really hot summer and the weir had completely dried up. You could see a wall running across the river, only a tiny layer of water covering it up. Autumn skipped across it and dared me to do the same.

I tried to say no, but like I said, Autumn doesn't really do 'no'. In the end, she held my hand and practically dragged me across. I clutched her hand so tightly she had red marks from my nails in her palm for a week.

It felt amazing once we got to the other side, so I was glad she'd insisted – as I usually am. I'd never do something like that of my own accord though. Never in a million years. It's not that I'm a complete wimp; just, well, it's dangerous! It might *look* safe, but you never know what's underneath or how slippy it is, or if the river will suddenly change and you'll get washed away and knocked unconscious on the rocks below.

Too risky by half, and the Green family doesn't do risky. We like things to be ordered, safe, predictable. That's why we come here. It's *always* predictable here. At least it always has been up to now.

D ad points to the mist swirling above the weir
as we pick our way across moss-covered
rocks. The water's crashing down so hard we
have to shout to hear each other. It's like Niagara Falls.

'Not surprising after all the rain we've had this summer!' Dad yells in my ear.

I stand back as some of the spray splashes a rock
below us. 'Let's go back!' I shout.

We pass Mr Andrews, one of Dad's friends, on the
way back to the apartment. I study the wood on the
other side of the river as they chat. Row after row of
tall, sturdy trees, they look proud and aloof, as if they
know more than we do. They've seen it all. The leaves
on a group of them have turned red. The same trees
every year, just one small section of the wood. How do
they do it? How do they know?

'Come on, treacle.' Dad nudges me and I give Mr
Andrews a quick wave and an embarrassed smile as
we set off. Will Dad *ever* realise I've grown out of his

pet names? Will I ever have the heart to tell him?

We go into the leisure centre so Dad can book a squash court for him and Mr Andrews. He never plays squash except when we're here; I don't know why he bothers. I watched a bit of his game once. He's really thin and spindly. He looked like a spider on ice, slipping about all over the court, crashing into walls and coming away purple with bruises. Mr Andrews had hardly built up a sweat.

Dad books the court for tomorrow afternoon and then stops to talk to the receptionist. I look round the mini-shop while they talk. There's a rail of tiny gym outfits and skimpy swimming costumes and six shelves of chocolates and sweets. I've never quite understood how the two go together.

'Just a little surprise for your mum,' Dad says, linking his arm through mine as he pockets a gift token for a facial.

It's their wedding anniversary tomorrow. Fifteen years. They still get all gooey about each other, and they hardly ever argue. They bicker sometimes, of course. But only as much as anyone's parents, and about a hundred times less than Autumn's. *Their* arguments are like volcanic eruptions. One minute they're so laid back they're practically lying down, and the next they're at each other's throats. Autumn says it's because they're artists. It's the creative temperament.

'If I could have your attention please.' Mr Barraclough taps the side of his glass with a spoon and the room gradually quietens. Mr Barraclough's the manager here. He's really tall, with a wavy mop of grey hair and blue eyes that always seem to shine without sparkling, if that makes sense.

He wears sharp suits and always has his shirt collar turned up. I think he looks like a cross between a faded popstar and a really cool headmaster. He calls himself the 'chief skivvy'.

Everyone's at the welcome meeting, looking up at him and waiting to hear about the week's goodies. Well, everyone except Autumn's family. They aren't here yet – but that's no surprise. They're late to everything! I think they like to make an entrance.

Mum eyes the drinks. 'Champagne this year,' she says raising her eyebrows. 'What's that about, then?'

I had champagne once, at Autumn's house. Her Mum had just put on a really successful show at the gallery with a mega-famous artist. Autumn said she'd drunk it before. I didn't like it all that much. It fizzed straight up into my nose and hurt, so I don't bother asking Mum if I can have a glass.

She pats her stomach. 'Shame I can't have one,' she says. I grab three cups of orange juice for her, Craig and myself as Dad helps himself to a glass of champagne and downs half of it in one gulp.

Mr Barraclough has started talking again. 'So, as this is my last year, I thought we'd splash out a bit,' he says.

'Bit young for retiring, aren't you?' a red-faced man

at the side of the room calls out. 'Or are we paying you too much?'

'I wish!' Mr Barraclough says, half frowning, half smiling. 'No, I just thought I'd go travelling. See a bit of the world beyond Riverside Village,' he adds. 'I'm fifty this year. Can't put your life on hold forever.' Then he stares out of the window and pauses. For a moment, he seems to have forgotten about all of us. The pause is just starting to feel awkward when he coughs and raises his glass with a smile that looks really sad. You'd think he'd seem a bit happier about packing in his job to go travelling!

'Anyway, I hope you all settle into your apartments without any problems,' he says. 'I'm here whenever you need me, as are my staff. Try to remember, if it's a sink you need unblocking, there's Johnny and Rita and Pete, and if you need someone to share a long drink and a chat in the bar, you've got my number.'

A few people laugh while Mr Barraclough takes a sip of his drink. 'We've laid on a whole host of top notch events for you this week, as always,' he carries on, 'so please take your time to check out all the activities, get yourself booked on before it's too late, and most of all, have a wonderful week. Thank you.'

With that, he raises his glass and nods his head to a small round of applause.

Mum grabs my arm. 'Come on, let's see what they've got planned.'

I grab a handful of dry-roasted peanuts and follow her to join the others crowding round a table that stretches down one side of the room. It's covered with leaflets and information sheets and booking forms. Dad and Craig wander over to a board at the other side of the room. It shows pictures of a local steam train. That's another thing that happens every year. Craig's world would be turned upside down if we didn't have at least one ride on the steam train while we're here.

'Look. They haven't done a trip here before, have they?' Mum passes me a leaflet about a candle museum that we've heard of but never visited. 'You can make your own candles,' she adds.

I study the leaflet. There are pictures of candles shaped like mermaids and fairies and trees and all sorts of things. I imagine Autumn and I making matching candles and giving them to each other as presents. 'It looks good,' I agree.

Mum picks up the booking sheet. 'They're doing a trip tomorrow afternoon. Shall I book us in?'

'Yeah, great,' I reply, glancing at the door for the twentieth time to see if Autumn's here yet.

A second later, Dad comes over, pulling Craig along by the hand. Craig's walking like a bow-legged cowboy; his trousers are soaked.

'He knocked his drink over,' Dad says. 'I'll take him home to change. Back in a minute.'

He pauses at the door to talk to someone who's just arrived. I peer round the corner. Yay! It's Autumn!

She screams my name so loud half the room turns to see what's going on, then she runs over and squeezes me so tightly she practically winds me, as her parents come in behind her. They're dressed in matching linen trousers and bright tops: his baby blue, hers bright pink. Autumn's wearing old jeans and a red t-shirt with a white donkey in the middle. When they come in, the room changes, as though it was black and white before, and they've flicked a switch that's turned it into colour.

'Didn't you girls see each other about two hours ago?' Mum asks.

'Yeah, but we've not had time to catch up on the two million things we need to tell each other yet,' Autumn says.

'Two million? It was a million and a half at the last count,' her mum says with a smile.

'That was two hours ago! There's more now!'

I laugh, but she's right. There's always so much I want to tell her. Just stupid things, stuff most people wouldn't bother with but I know she'll want to know about.

'I suppose I know what you mean,' Mum says, kissing Autumn's mum on the cheek and pulling her to one side while Autumn's dad goes over to speak to Mr Barraclough.

'Let's see what they've got lined up for us then,' Autumn says with a wink as she snatches up a handful of leaflets. 'Nope, nope, nah, no way,' she says, quickly scanning each one before dropping it back down and moving along the table.

'Candles!' she snorts, throwing down the leaflet Mum and I had been looking at. 'Who'd want to go and visit a candle museum? I mean, *please!*'

I don't say anything as I shuffle some papers on the table so she can't see the booking sheet – and I turn away so she doesn't see my pink cheeks either. Suddenly, Autumn's by my side, pulling on my arms and jigging up and down like a toddler. 'Look at this, Jenni,' she says.

It's a brochure for an outdoor adventure centre in a village about ten miles away.

'We've got to go!' Autumn says. 'Listen to this. They do rock climbing, abseiling, assault courses, all sorts.'

I *knew* she'd try and talk me into something like this. 'I don't know,' I murmur, playing for time. I mean I know it generally feels great *after* I've done some scary stunt that Autumn's persuaded me is a good idea – but that doesn't mean I'm desperate for the next one! 'Abseiling? Rock climbing? Don't those involve heights?' I ask nervously. 'I mean – don't you think it could be a bit dangerous?'

'And horse riding! That's it – we're going!' Autumn bursts out, instantly clicking her teeth and jumping around me, trotting like a horse. 'Remember the wooden horses we had in Year Two, Jen?'

We'd persuaded our parents to buy us matching hobby horses and we used to trit-trot *everywhere* on them. We pretended we were cowgirls out on the desert plains hunting for long lost treasure.

I laugh. 'Mm, but like you say, we were in Year Two – and they *were* wooden. No danger of having one of them trample on your feet!'

Autumn stops trotting and turns to look for her

mum. She's standing in the middle of the room, her hand on my mum's stomach, smiling as they talk.

'What's going on?' I ask, as we join them.

'He kicked,' Mum says, beaming.

'He?' Mrs Leonard asks, raising an eyebrow.

'Well, we don't know for sure,' Mum says, 'but he feels like a he to me. Feel the kick on those legs and tell me we haven't got a little footballer in there!'

I reach out to touch Mum's stomach. A tiny thump pushes at my hand. It fills my heart to think there's a little life in there. My little baby brother. I can't wait to meet him.

Autumn puts her hand next to mine. 'AWESOME!' she yells. Then she bends down and talks directly to Mum's stomach. 'Hey, Jenni's little bro,' she says. 'Please will you tell Mrs Green that Jenni and I are going horse riding?'

'What's that?' her mum asks.

Autumn opens up the brochure. 'Horse riding! We're going on the trip tomorrow!' she announces. Autumn doesn't generally do requests. There'd be no point; no one ever says no to her.

'It's on tomorrow?' I falter. 'But I've just signed up for the trip to . . . ' My voice trails off.

'They only do the horse riding on Sundays,' Autumn says, studying the brochure. She started riding lessons this year and thinks it's the best thing ever. I went with her once. I didn't like it all that much, even though I knew I probably should. All girls my age love horses, but I just think they're so . . . well, big! My favourite

23

animals are generally the type you can cuddle without worrying about them standing on your feet and crushing your toes to dust. Cute fluffy ones like puppies and kittens.

'Mum, we can go, can't we?' Autumn persists.

'I don't see why not,' her mum answers, looking at the times of the class. 'As long as you can get a lift back. We could drop you off but your Dad's booked us both in for an aromatherapy massage later on.' She turns to my mum. 'Can you pick them up?'

'I thought you wanted to go to the candle museum, Jenni?' Mum says.

Autumn bursts out laughing as my cheeks heat up.

'I was only doing it for you,' I say quickly. 'You go with Craig. I'd rather go horse riding.' And it's true. Suddenly the idea of a candle museum sounds dull to me, too. Even if horse riding *is* a bit scary, if Autumn's there I know it'll be more fun than anything else I could be doing.

And anyway, both of us want to be together as often as possible this week as we're not going to see each other as much once we get home. We go to different secondary schools. I go to the local comprehensive and she goes to a grammar school in the next town. Autumn went through months of agony last year, trying to decide where to go. She wanted to be with me, but her dream is to be a famous artist, and everyone said that she should go there, as it's got a brilliant art department. Even I agreed – reluctantly. And apart from missing each other, we're both really happy where we are.

We've always promised each other that it won't

change anything between us and that we'll be best friends forever. So far, that seems to be the case. But now it's the start of another year, I can't help worrying a little. I mean, you never *really* know what's going to happen, do you?

Wouldn't it be great if you did, though? If you could just have a little glimpse of what the future holds. Just so you'd know. That would be so cool.

'All right, love. Your Dad can pick you up,' Mum says with a smile. 'I'm sure he won't want to be dragged round a boring museum, either.'

'Thanks Mum,' I say as Autumn grabs my hand and drags me off.

We pass Dad and Craig coming back in as we leave. 'Don't be late in,' Dad calls after us. 'I thought we'd all have a game of Monopoly before Craig's bed time.'

Autumn laughs as she runs outside. 'Honestly, Jen. Monopoly? It's non-stop thrills with your family!' Then she pinches me, tickling me till I fall to the ground laughing hysterically.

Two girls are walking towards us as we chase each other down the path: Christine and Sally. They've been coming here as long as we have. They're about our age, but as different from us as you can get. Both perfect and pretty, with their long blonde hair and little pink handbags swinging on their arms. Their pace quickens and their smiles widen when they spot us. Correction: when they spot *Autumn*.

'Hi!' they enthuse in unison, crowding round Autumn and hardly noticing me.

'You want to hang out with us tomorrow?' Christine asks. 'I've got some new straighteners we can try out on each other, or we could go shopping or something.' Both girls hold their breath while they wait for Autumn to answer. It's like being best friends with a pop star. Everyone always wants to know Autumn.

'Sorry, we're out tomorrow,' Autumn says lazily. I don't think she even realises how much everyone craves her company. 'Catch up with you later in the week maybe.'

The girls try not to show their disappointment. 'Cool,' Sally says. 'See you later.'

'Bye, then!' I say pointedly as they turn away.

'Oh, see you Jenni,' Christine calls over her shoulder as an afterthought.

Autumn nudges me once they're out of sight. 'Why would I want to hang out with Barbie One and Barbie Two, anyway?' she says.

'Autumn, that's mean!' I say, secretly trying not to smile as we head back down the path, away from the apartments, along the river, and across the long bridge that curves over to a field on the other side.

A bit further up, the river opens out into its widest stretch. It's almost a lake, virtually still and shallow. If you watch closely, you can just about see the current slinking forwards.

Across the bridge, you can creep round some bushes at the very edge of the lake to a tiny rocky bay hidden round the corner. It's our secret place.

Autumn kicks off her shoes and rolls up her trousers.

Splashing into the water, she picks up a stone and skims it across the lake. It bounces six times. 'Oh, yes! The stone skimming champion of the world strikes again!' she whoops.

I edge into the water behind her. It's freezing.

'So what's new?' she asks, scavenging for another flat stone. 'Any gossip?'

I laugh. 'Gossip? Me? *You're* the one with the exciting life!'

'That's true,' she says as she flicks her stone across the lake.

'Oi!' I laugh, kicking water at her.

She bends down to splash me. Laughing and screaming, we chase each other back to the pebbly cove.

Autumn flops down on the stones. 'Come on,' she says, rubbing her feet with her sleeve and putting her shoes back on.

'We've just got here.'

'Let's go down to the weir, see how full it is.'

'It's full. I've seen it.'

'Yeah, but not with me, you haven't.'

That's how it is with Autumn. As soon as we're doing one thing, she's ready to move on to something else. I follow her as she dances along the path. On the way, I tell her about Craig being sick on the way up, and about the book I'm reading, and I point out the leaves that have gone red like they always do. Silly stuff, really, but there's something about sharing things with Autumn that's important. As though nothing's quite real until I have.

It's just starting to get dark when we get back to the apartments. The steam train puffs through the woods across the river, letting out its comic little 'Toot!' before it disappears under a bridge.

'I wouldn't believe that train was for real if we hadn't actually been on it,' Autumn says. 'It's like something out of a cartoon.'

'Yep. It's definitely real,' I say, remembering last year when Craig and Mikey stuck their heads out of the window and tooted at the tops of their voices, making an elderly lady jump out of her skin. I thought they'd given her a heart attack.

'It's all so organised here, isn't it?' Autumn continues. 'Not like normal life.'

'It's certainly nothing like *your* life!' I say with a laugh. '*Nothing's* organised at your house!'

'Don't you ever think it's not like the real world here?' Autumn grabs my arm, her eyes dancing. She hops backwards as she talks. 'Hey, maybe it's an alternate universe!' Her tone gets higher, her eyes become even more animated. 'Or a film! Maybe we're in a movie and we don't even know! Like the one where that guy keeps living the exact same day over and over again.'

'Or the one where he finds out that his whole life is really a television programme?'

'That's it! Nothing's real up here. It's all just a TV

show!' Autumn leaps behind a bush, pretending to hold a camera as she jumps out next to me, filming me as I walk along.

'Yeah, right,' I laugh. 'Who'd want to make a film of *me*?'

Autumn carries on filming. 'Maybe you're not really you but a clone of yourself and the real you is carrying on a parallel life somewhere else!'

A cold shiver flashes up my back and neck. What if something like that was really possible? Then I laugh. 'You've been reading too many sci–fi books,' I say.

Autumn pretends to throw the camera over her shoulder. 'You're right,' she laughs. 'Did I tell you about the one I'm reading now?'

And the conversation's forgotten as she recounts the story of a boy who lives his whole life not knowing that he's a clone of his dead brother. Creepy.

We've reached her block.

'You coming in?'

'I'd better get back,' I say. 'Dad'll start moaning if I'm not in soon.'

'See you tomorrow then,' Autumn calls as she pushes the big glass door open. 'Enjoy Monopoly!' She blows me an elaborate kiss and waves as I leave.

But once I'm outside, I hear a loud clanking noise from inside, like something falling. Autumn!

I run into the foyer. It's all marble and water features. Autumn's block is different from the others: fancier, and older. The lift's on one side, next to another, older lift that doesn't work, and there's a big arch leading to the ground floor corridor opposite. An ornate mirror hangs on the wall across from the entrance, in between a couple of other doors. One of them is open.

'Hello?' I call. 'Autumn?'

No answer. She's gone; there's no one around, and there's nothing out of place either. I turn to leave, but just as I'm about to open the door, I look back to see someone coming out of the old lift. He's got a pile of logs in his arms, so high I can't see his face, and an axe gripped under his elbow. Must be the caretaker.

But then I notice his hair over the top of the logs. It's Mr Barraclough! What's he doing here? I mean, I know he does do a few odd jobs around the place – doesn't mind 'rolling up his sleeves' as he puts it – but what's he doing in the lift?

It's one of those really old-fashioned ones with a big metal gate that you have to pull across. It's never worked, as far as I know, and it's just used as a storage cupboard. The new lift next to it works fine so I don't think anyone's ever bothered to try to get it working.

'Hi,' I say from the doorway. As he glances up at me, a couple of logs fall from his arms.

'Drat,' he mutters, bending to pick them up, but dropping more in the process.

'Can I help?' I ask, hurrying to pick the logs up for him.

'Thanks.' He points to the open door. 'I'm transferring all these things into that cupboard.'

'Why are you doing that?' I ask, dropping the logs on to a shelf in the cupboard.

Mr Barraclough shakes his head slowly as he returns to the old lift for another stash. 'Good question,' he says, his voice cracking slightly. Almost in a whisper, he adds, 'Trying to get the old thing working, like the silly fool that I am.' He gets a spanner out of his pocket and waves it at me. 'Broken wires you see. Thought I'd have a go at fixing them. Silly stories,' he says with a laugh. 'But you never know. It just might have . . . ' His voice fades away. He doesn't look at me as he speaks. It doesn't even feel as though he's talking to me.

He stands there looking down at his feet till I start to feel a bit itchy. Has he lost his mind? He's not making the slightest bit of sense.

'Um, I'd better be . . . um . . . ' I point to the entrance, my voice trailing away.

Mr Barraclough suddenly seems to remember I'm there. 'Yes, of course.' He fixes a quick smile in my direction. 'Sorry. Ignore me – silly old fool. Thanks for your help. Off you go, now.'

'Right. Bye,' I say before I scurry away, wondering if perhaps he'd had a tad too much champagne at the welcome meeting. It was as though he'd slipped off into another world – a bit like he did at the meeting too.

And I don't know if it's because of the sci-fi story or all those things Autumn was talking about, but the thought suddenly fires up my imagination. What if we *could* slip into another world, just by thinking about it? What if we could travel into a different dimension whenever we wanted, travel through space and time with a click of the fingers? How cool would that be?

For a second, the idea grips me so hard it makes my whole body twitch and prickle and I can't wait to share it with Autumn. But when I try to imagine putting it into words, the idea seems to dissolve and slip away from me, and a moment later, I can't recapture it at all.

As I walk back to our apartment, I laugh at myself. That's what hanging out with Autumn does to you; makes you start believing in impossible things. I mean, fantasy worlds and different dimensions – as if!

3

Mum pokes her head round the door.

'Jenni, are you going to have some breakfast?'

'I'll be with you in a bit,' I groan. She takes this as an invitation to come in and open the curtains. A chink of bright light cuts across the room. '*Mum!*' I pull the covers further over my head.

'Come on then, we want to sort out our plans for the day,' she says as she closes the door behind her.

I don't normally lie in. It's this place. It always takes me hours to get to sleep on the first night. You can hear the river running past, right outside the window. At home, we live near a railway. I can quite happily sleep through the goods trains going past three times a night, but a river? Too noisy.

Once I do get to sleep, it always seems much deeper here. I have vivid technicolour dreams, and then I wake up in a bit of a daze and can't drag myself out of bed.

I reach for my diary. I never start my day without writing at least three pages. When I finally make it into the living room, it's nearly eleven o'clock. Craig's sitting cross-legged on the floor about ten centimetres away from the television, watching a cartoon. Mum's on the sofa with the Sunday newspaper spread out around her. Dad's washing up.

'Afternoon,' Dad says without looking up.

'Sorry, couldn't wake up,' I say as I pour some cereal into a bowl. 'Happy anniversary,' I add, handing Mum a card.

'Oh, sweetheart, that's nice of you,' she smiles. Dad dries his hands and joins her on the sofa so they can open the card together. It's got two teddy bears on it, sitting in a boat.

'Thanks, sweet pea,' Dad says with a wink before going back to the washing-up.

'So, shall we sort the day out, now we're all here?' Mum asks. 'We've got the restaurant booked for tonight, haven't we Tom?'

Dad nods. Their anniversary dinner. They always go to this posh restaurant to celebrate. Usually, someone babysits for me and Craig but Mum insists we all go this year. She wants it to be a celebration of the family, she says, not just her and Dad. I guess it's with the little one on the way – this is one of the last times going out as a family will mean just the four of us.

'I'm going horse riding this afternoon, remember,' I call from the table as I shovel cereal into my mouth.

'And I'm playing squash,' Dad calls from the sink.

'What time?' Mum asks.

'Four fifteen, why?'

Mum turns to me. 'What time does horse riding finish, Jenni?'

'Half four.'

'Well, that's it then,' she says to Dad. 'You'll have to cancel squash.'

'What? How d'you work that out?'

'I told Autumn's parents we'd collect the girls. They're dropping them off, it's only fair.'

'Oh no! Can't you pick them up, love?'

'I'm going on the candle museum tour with Craig. I signed up for it.'

'Well, I signed up for squash,' Dad says. He dries his hands on a tea towel and comes back to the sofa to snuggle up with Mum. He tickles her cheek and kisses her neck. 'I think you might even find that I signed up for squash first,' he says. 'Although if it's too much for you . . . '

Mum slaps his hand away from her cheek. 'I don't really know why you bother with squash. It's not as though you're any good at it,' she says, laughing.

'Oi!' He tickles her harder, till Mum begs him to stop.

'OK, OK, I'll do it!' she screeches eventually.

Dad turns serious. 'Are you sure? I mean, you're definitely up to it?'

'I'm only pregnant; I'm not incapacitated,' she says. 'It's fine. I'll take Craig to the museum in the car and then we won't have to wait for the coach back.'

'Look, neither of you needs to cancel anything,' I say. 'We *can* get a bus you know.'

'No you can't,' Dad says. 'Not on your own.'

'Dad, I'm twelve. I'm not a baby.'

'I know, sweet pea, but it's a long way, and you've never been before. We don't even know if there *is* a bus.

'I'll fetch you. It's fine, honestly,' Mum says.

I rinse my bowl. Why do they always have to treat me like a little kid? I suddenly feel crowded and claustrophobic. 'I'm going to see Autumn.'

'Do you need to spend *every* minute with Autumn?' Dad asks. 'You're seeing her this afternoon.' He gets up off the sofa to follow me out of the room. 'I had actually wondered if we might all go out for a walk this morning.' He nearly trips over Craig, still motionless on the floor, his jaw open, eyes fixed on cartoon aliens. 'Craig, you've watched enough of that,' Dad says. 'Turn it off, now.'

'It's just getting to a good bit,' Craig whines.

'I said *off.*' Dad walks over to the telly and switches it off.

Craig instantly breaks into a wail. He sounds like an air raid siren.

'I'm outta here,' I say, heading for the door. I pause. 'Is that OK? Maybe we can have a walk later?'

Dad lets out a breath. 'Never mind. I'll take Craig, and your mum can have a rest.'

'Do I have to?' Craig bleats. 'Can't I go with Jenni?'

'No, you can't,' I say. The last thing I want right now is my little brother snapping at my heels.

'I'll be back in a bit,' I add and head over to Autumn's block.

I stand in her foyer, waiting for the lift, frustrated and fed up. It isn't coming. I've pressed the button, but nothing's happening. The stairs are right over the other side of the building so I hardly ever use them. A young couple pass me, holding hands and smiling into each other's eyes as they leave the building. They don't even notice me. I bet they're here on their honeymoon.

What's the matter with the lift?

I'll have to use the stairs. I need to be with Autumn. She's the only person who understands me. I mean my family's all right, as families go. But it's still a family, isn't it? Still parents who treat you like you're a little kid and don't trust you to do anything yourself.

I wish I was older. I could do what I wanted then. Go where I like whenever I felt like it.

Just as I'm thinking this, I pass the old lift, the one that's never worked. I bang my fist on its door. 'Stupid lift,' I say.

And then I hear something. A whirring noise, and a thumping and banging from inside the lift. Then a tapping noise, getting louder, coming nearer! I stand back. Finally – CLANK! What's that? Has Mr Barraclough fixed the lift after all?

The noise stops.

I look around me. What harm could it do? I pull the heavy metal door open. Behind it, there's another door, also metal, with concertina brass bars ridged across it, like a gate.

I pull it across and enter the lift. It's so old and run down, I don't believe for a minute it could work. What if I get inside and it plummets down for miles, taking me with it?

I laugh at myself. Sometimes my imagination really does work overtime. It's not going to plummet anywhere. Besides, it's not as if the other one looks like it's coming – and I've always found this lift fascinating.

There are four black buttons on the wall: *3, 2, 1* and *G*. Underneath the buttons, a piece of plywood is nailed to the wall; above them there's a bright red button with 'ALARM' written beside it. Above that, a notice says 'Please close both doors as you exit the lift. Thank you.'

I pull the outer door closed; then slide the gate across, shutting out the light except for a tiny sliver poking through the grated window in the door.

I've never been in an old-fashioned lift like this before. It makes me feel as though I'm in an old spy movie. Maybe Autumn and I could invent a story about it. I make a mental note to add it to my list of things I want to talk to her about.

And then I press the button for the first floor.

For a moment, nothing happens. I wait in the gloom as a tiny ball of panic starts to uncurl in my stomach. Why didn't I just go round to the stairs?

And then it moves. Clunking into action, it judders

upwards, scraping and rumbling to the next floor. Then, with a giant THUD that makes my teeth rattle, it jumps to a halt.

I heave the doors open and leave the lift behind.

Autumn's apartment is right at the end of the corridor. I knock our special rap on the door. *Tap tappity tap tap*, pause, *tap tap*.

Nothing.

I knock again and then peer over the balcony to the car park. Three cars down there, but not Autumn's. You don't easily miss a bright red Porsche. Where are they? I bang heavily on the door one last time before giving up and turning away.

I run down the stairs this time and out to the front of the apartments. For a second, I think I hear Autumn's voice and I stop and listen, but I don't hear it again. Maybe they've gone out for the morning.

I try our place by the lake, but someone else is there. A group of young kids and two sets of parents. That's *our* place! But I don't stop to argue with them. It's not as if there's a law against other people going there!

The bay looks bigger than yesterday. It seems to reach further across the lake, a whole beach of grey and white stones. Strange.

Maybe she's at the weir. I run down there and call her name. Two teenage lads are messing about on the rocks. They seem to be trying to cross the weir. They must be nuts! It's so high at the moment, they're bound to kill themselves. I edge towards them. That's when I see something *really* odd. The weir, it's not rushing and

39

gushing over the top like Niagara Falls any more. It's more like a little stream, a slow, shallow dribble over the long wall that stretches across the river.

How did that happen? I suppose it hasn't rained overnight. Is that all it takes to make the difference?

On the way back to our apartment, I have a quick look in the leisure centre. Maybe Autumn and her family have gone for a swim. Of course – they'll be in there. Bound to be, especially as we didn't have any plans till this afternoon. No one in that family ever sits down for longer than half a minute.

But they're not there. They must have gone for a walk or something.

Without telling me?

I decide to try their apartment one last time. My frustration seems to have given me energy, and I've wandered round to the other side of their building by now, so I run up the stairs and march down the corridor to their apartment.

Tap tappity tap tap. Tap tap.

Come on, Autumn. Be in. I don't want to have to go home just yet.

There's a noise behind the door. 'Who is it?' a voice calls. A strange voice. Pleasant and sweet, it reminds me of a bird call – but it's not the voice of anyone in Autumn's family.

'It's me,' I call back, slightly uncertainly. 'Jenni.'

'Jenni who?' the voice sings back to me.

'Jenni! Um . . . Do you want to let me in?' I ask, even more uncertainly. Whose voice *is* that?

The door opens. A woman I've never seen in my life is holding on to the handle. Probably in her fifties, she's got greying hair tied back in a pony tail and she's wearing a long, floaty red dress and gold flip-flops. She smiles at me. 'Can I help you, dear?' she asks.

'Who are you?' I gasp, stepping back to check the door. Apartment 110. Autumn's apartment.

'Who are *you*?' the woman retorts.

'Autumn's friend.'

'Autumn's friend? What does that mean?'

'My friend's parents own this apartment.'

'I'm afraid they don't. This is my apartment. You must have made a mistake dear. Sorry.' She smiles kindly at me and moves to close the door.

'Wait!' The woman pauses, the door open just wide enough so I can see her eyes. 'Have you definitely got the right week?' I ask. 'They own it on week 35. Are you just leaving?' My questions don't make sense, even to me. She can't be leaving! They've already arrived. They got here last night. 'Are you staying with them?' I ask, searching my memory to work out who she could be. I've met Autumn's gran. It's not her. A friend of the family?

'I've told you, love,' the woman says. 'This is my apartment, my week. I arrived yesterday; I don't know anything about your friend.' She smiles again, slightly more woodenly this time. 'Like I say, I'm ever so sorry I can't help you. Now, if you don't mind, I could do with getting back to my needlework. Is there anything else?'

'I . . .'

The woman waits a bit longer.

'Well, all right then,' she says. 'I'll be going. Sorry again dear. Hope you find your friend.' And with that, she closes the door.

I stare at the number. 110. I trace each digit with my fingers. One, one, zero. It *is* their apartment. Am I going mad?

Finally, I turn to go home, walking blindly down the corridor, completely shaken. The old lift is standing open, waiting for me. I walk into it in a complete daze, close the outer door, pull the metal gate across and hit the button for the ground floor. All the way home, I go over what just happened, arguing and reasoning with myself to try and make it make sense. I must have got the wrong apartment. Maybe they changed it without telling me. They *must* have done. Or I went to the wrong floor by mistake.

By the time I get back to our apartment, I've just about managed to convince myself that the whole thing was my own stupid mistake. Nothing to worry about at all. I'm not losing my mind. There'll be a simple explanation. There's got to be.

D ad's hunched over the living room table, writing. 'Autumn's been looking for you,' he says without looking up.

'What? She's been here?'

'You just missed her. Left five minutes ago. Maybe ten. Said she'd been looking all over for you. Listen, what d'you think of this? "The river raced ruggedly down the hill, falling over itself as though it was in a hurry." ' He looks up. 'It's the opening of my novel.'

'It's great, Dad. I thought you'd already begun your novel.'

Dad leans back over his notebook. 'Starting a new one. I just got a fresh idea. It's this place. Inspires me. We should come here more often.'

I get some orange juice from the fridge. 'Did Autumn say where she was going?'

'Back to her apartment.'

'Back to her apartment?'

'That's what I said.'

'And she left ten minutes ago?' I sip my juice.

'Correct.'

'Dad, have they swapped their apartment?' I was at her place less than ten minutes ago – and she wasn't there. I *must* have got the wrong one!

'Good grief Jen, what's with the Spanish Inquisition? Not that I know of. Why don't you ask her when she comes round? She said she's coming back in a bit.'

Of course. I'll just ask her. There'll be a simple explanation. 'Where's Mum?' I ask.

'Taken Craig for a swim.'

'Are they—'

'Look, Jenni, I'm just trying to do a bit of work. I'm not being funny but do you mind . . . ?'

I shake my head as I wash my glass out in the sink. Let him convince himself he's writing an internationally bestselling blockbuster.

Something catches my eye outside the window and I look up. Autumn. At last! I run to the door to let her in.

'Where've you *been*?' we squeal in unison before I grab her arm and drag her inside.

'Hi, Mr Green,' she calls through the door. Dad waves a hand absent-mindedly in reply. We go upstairs to my room and I close the door behind us. 'I couldn't find you anywhere – it was like you'd disappeared into thin air!' Autumn says.

'I know! What on earth happened?'

'Spooky!' she says, laughing, and pretending to play creepy music on a piano in mid-air.

'I know. Completely bizarre. I couldn't make any

sense of it at first, but I've realised I must have just made a mistake with your apartment.'

'My apartment?'

'Yeah. When did you change it?'

'Change what?' Autumn tilts her head at me, waiting for me to explain.

'The . . . the . . . your . . . apartment?' I falter.

'We haven't changed the apartment,' Autumn says, screwing up her nose at me.

'And your car,' I add, feeling like a right idiot. 'It wasn't there.'

'Course it was, you nana!' Autumn says. Then she half covers her eyes and walks round the room banging into things. 'You must have been walking round with blinkers on.'

She walks into the side of the bed and does this really over the top fall on to it, making me laugh. She's right – it was obviously just me being stupid. It must have been. I force it out of my mind and convince myself that there'll be an explanation.

'Hey, I've got you a present,' she says, sitting up and pulling something out of her pocket. 'Close your eyes and hold out your hand.'

I do as she says and she places something on to my palm. I close my hand around it.

'Open your eyes!'

It's a necklace made from some pebbles with wire mesh holding them in place. It's lovely, and unusual: exactly the kind of thing Autumn does – and the kind of thing that makes her so amazing!

'I made it last night,' she says, grinning broadly. 'They're from our place. It's a friendship necklace.'

I sit down next to her and hug her. 'I love it. Thank you.' Autumn watches me as I tie it round my neck.

'You're welcome,' she says, jumping off the bed. 'So – tell me more about the weird stuff. Maybe you weren't walking round with blinkers on after all. Maybe our car was abducted by aliens.'

'What would aliens want with a bright red Porsche?' I ask, laughing.

'Maybe they're going to turn it into a spaceship and use it for races between their planet and ours?' She goes over to the French window and opens it up. The river roars loudly past.

'Or maybe they come from a planet where every-thing's red,' I say. 'Bit by bit, they're going to steal all the red things from our planet.'

Autumn jumps up and down and claps her hands. 'Yeah that's it!' she exclaims. 'Yay – no more beetroot!'

'No more tomatoes!'

'Oh.' Autumn slumps back on to the bed, the smile gone.

'What is it?' I ask.

'No more tomato ketchup,' she says glumly. An instant later, she brightens up again. 'Oh well – we'll just have to hope it's not the aliens at all and that it was just you not noticing our car.'

I pause for a moment, remembering all the other things that were different. 'No, it was more than that,' I say tentatively.

'Like what?' Autumn looks intensely into my eyes. Then she glances round the room. Picking up one of my trainers, she shoves it under the bed. 'Lost your shoes as well did you?' Then she puts on a fake mysterious voice. 'Hey,' she says, pointing at the floor, 'I'm sure there was a shoe down there before. It's such a mystery!'

I laugh and shove her on to the bed. 'No, really. It was *definitely* more than that,' I say seriously. 'Where were you anyway?'

Autumn shrugs. 'The lake, the weir, at home, looking for you.'

All the same places I'd been. How could we have missed each other at every place?

'Autumn.'

She's reaching under the bed, fiddling with the arm of one of Craig's discarded robots. It comes off in her hand. 'Uh huh?'

'It was strange. I don't know how to explain it.'

'Ooh goody!' Autumn puts down the robot and crosses her legs. 'Come on, then. Tell me more.'

'Only if you promise not to make fun of me.'

Autumn pulls an ultra-serious face. 'I promise,' she says solemnly.

So I tell her about going to her apartment, and about the woman in the floaty dress and how I couldn't see Autumn or her family anywhere.

'Cool!' she says. 'I must have turned invisible!'

'I'm being serious!'

'*I'm* being serious. What other explanation is there?'

'Autumn, you seriously think you've become invisible?'

'Why not? If you can clone people and you can find out your whole life is a TV programme, what makes you so convinced you can't become invisible?'

'Autumn, those were stories!'

'Who says this isn't?'

I pick up some Lego from the floor and throw it on to Craig's bed. Why does he have to make such a mess? 'How come Dad could see you, then?' I ask. 'And what about the woman in the apartment? And where was your car?'

'I said. Been there all morning,' Autumn says. 'You did go to the right place, didn't you?'

'Block C, 110. End apartment, first floor.'

'Yep, that's us.' Autumn jumps off the bed and bounds over to the window again. It's started raining, fat splodges squashing lazily against the glass. She pulls the French window closed and stands looking out. 'OK, I can't explain that,' she says finally.

'I must have got it wrong,' I say. 'Had a brain drain. I did. I went to the wrong apartment, I'm sure of it now.' I don't know who I'm more determined to convince – Autumn or myself. Autumn seems happy enough with my conclusion – even if I'm not so sure. Seeing as I don't have a better explanation, I decide to ignore the bit of my brain that's silently trying to argue against my words.

'Well, that's that sorted then,' Autumn says, turning round. 'And I suppose we probably just kept missing each other. I guess I didn't go invisible after all.'

'I guess.'

'Shame.'

'Yeah.'

The front door bangs. 'We're home!' Mum calls.

Autumn jumps off the bed and glances at her watch. 'I need to be getting back for lunch in a minute. Come round at two, OK?'

'OK.'

Autumn pokes her head into the living room as we pass. 'Hi, Mrs Green.'

'Hi, Autumn,' Mum replies as she hangs Craig's towel over the radiator.

'Did you swim?' I ask.

Mum smiles and pats her stomach. 'With this? It'd be like a blue whale getting in the pool!'

'We saw workmen with a digger, and they talked to us and Mum said I can go back and watch them work tomorrow, didn't you Mum?' Craig tells us eagerly.

Mum ruffles his wet hair. 'Yes, darling.'

'OK guys, I'll catch you later, OK?' Autumn says, glancing at the clock. 'I gotta go.'

I see her to the door. 'See ya!' she says. And with that, she dances down the drive, pausing just before she goes out of sight to wave and blow me her usual flamboyant kiss. 'We're leaving at two on the dot,' she calls. 'Don't be late.'

'I won't.'

'Apartment 110!'

'Yes, don't worry. I'll come to the right place this time,' I force a laugh.

Once she's out of sight, I turn back to go inside, closing the door behind me.

'Jenni, lay the table for your mum,' Dad says. He's still sitting at the table.

'You'll have to move, then.'

'In a minute. Can't stop when it's flowing. You've heard of the person from Porlock haven't you?'

'Yes, Dad. We've all heard of the person from Porlock.'

He tells us this story about once a week. Some guy was writing a poem or something and he was interrupted by someone at the door: the person from Porlock. And that was the end of that. His inspiration was broken and the poem was never completed. It would have been a brilliant work of genius, and he never finished it. Great story. It's basically Dad's way of getting out of doing anything around the house.

'OK, lunch.' Mum brings a tray of sandwiches to the table, as I get the plates.

Dad leans across to kiss her. She touches the back of his head, holding him close to her. When they move apart, they smile at each other. He kisses her cheek. 'Fifteen years. Who'd have thought it, Mrs Green?' Dad says.

Mum smiles and leans down to rest her head on his shoulder. Then Dad gets up to clear away his notebooks. 'Come on, Craig.' Craig's in front of the telly again. 'Lunch.'

Normality. Thank goodness for that. For a moment, I forget all about the weird things and almost manage to convince myself they didn't happen. Life is calm and peaceful again, as it should be. As it always is. The normal, predictable Green family household – just how we like it.

As I enter Autumn's block, the old lift is standing open. I'm sure I closed it behind me. It's as though it saw me coming and opened specially!

The other one doesn't come when I call it, so I step inside and go up to the first floor. With the slightest jitter in my stomach, I stand outside apartment 110, staring at the door. 110. *Definitely* Autumn's apartment! I straighten my clothes. My top feels tight. Maybe I shouldn't have had a whole grab bag of crisps with my lunch.

I knock on the door.

'Who is it?'

Oh no! It's her again! But it *can't* be! This is the right place; I checked and double checked. What is going *on*?

The door opens a fraction.

'I'm sorry, I …'

The woman stares blankly at me for a split second, and then registers recognition. 'You again,' she says quietly. 'What do you want with me now?' She's not as friendly as last time. Her voice has an edge to it that could just be irritation but almost sounds scared.

'I'm just looking for Autumn,' I say.

'What do you mean, looking for Autumn? How do you lose a season?'

As she says this, her face suddenly drains of all colour. She pushes the door further closed – her eyes big and shocked against her suddenly grey face. When she talks again, it's as though she's looking straight through me and talking to a ghost.

'You're trying to make a fool of me, aren't you?' she says. 'You know! But how? It's impossible. No one knows – no one *ever* knew. Only me. Always lost.'

What's she talking about? 'I – I don't know what you mean,' I say, trying to sound as reasonable and un-threatening as I possibly can. 'I'm not trying to do anything bad, I just want to find Autumn. We're going out in a minute.'

The woman has stopped staring beyond me and seems to have remembered I'm here. 'Look.' She reaches a thin arm through the crack and points to the numbers on the door. '110. My apartment. My week. How many times do you need to be told?'

I can feel my eyes sting. 'I don't know,' I say. 'I don't *know* how many times I need to be told. All I know is that it doesn't make sense!'

The woman stares at me, holding my eyes for so long that I want to turn away, but the link between us feels so strong it's like a magnet and I can't move a muscle. 'What doesn't make sense?' she asks eventually.

'This is Autumn's apartment. I'm sure it is. They've been here for the last three years. I saw her half an hour ago!'

She stares a bit longer, as though she's trying to read my mind. That's when I realise – it's a joke! She's going to tell me, any second. It's Autumn messing about. I should have known she'd do something like this. She loves pranks!

'This is a joke, isn't it?' I say, feeling my body relax with relief as I smile at her.

'I thought as much,' the woman says. 'Look, I don't know where you got your facts, but it's not funny.'

'No – ' I try to backtrack. 'I mean – I thought you were playing a joke on me.'

The woman lets out a harsh laugh. '*Me* playing a joke on *you*?' she snaps. Then she shakes her head. 'You need to go now,' she says. 'Or I'm calling the police.'

And with that, she closes the door.

I try knocking again.

'I mean it,' she shouts through the door, her voice shaking. 'I'll phone them. You'll be in trouble.'

I can't stay here; things are just going from bad to worse. I check my watch. Gone two o' clock. They're going to leave without me.

A man I vaguely recognise is going into an apartment at the end of the corridor. I think he's a friend of Mr Leonard's.

'S'cuse me!' I call. He turns round and I run to catch up with him. 'I'm looking for Autumn,' I say.

'Autumn?'

'The Leonards, you know. Autumn and Mikey and their parents. They have an apartment in this block. Don't you know her dad?'

'Well, yes. I do. But . . . ' The man gives me a really weird look. As though I'm a bit simple and shouldn't be allowed to wander around on my own. He fiddles with the strap of his bag and slings it over his shoulder.

'Have you seen them?' I ask, a bit impatiently. Any second now I'm going to be too late. They've probably gone without me already. It's nearly quarter past two.

'Well, I've not seen them up here,' he says. 'Have you tried their apartment?'

'I've just *been* there!' I cry, frustration burning into my throat. 'They're not there. There's just this woman I've never seen before. Didn't you see us in the corridor?'

'How could I have seen you?' he laughs. 'I haven't been downstairs.'

'Huh? But we were there a second ago. Just over there.' Why is everyone talking in riddles to me today? What's going *on* here?

The man takes his bag off his shoulder and puts it down. He draws in a breath, then kind of puffs his cheeks out and looks away.

'What is it?' I ask.

'Have you seen the family recently?' His face is grim.

'Yes!' I scream. 'I was with Autumn half an hour ago and we're meant to be going out together. I've probably missed them now. Where are they? Do you know?'

'Listen. Why don't you just try their apartment again?'

'But I've just been there! I keep telling you! No one's come or gone since we've been standing here!'

'How do you know?'

54

'Because we'd have seen them!' What is this man's *problem*? 'Look, thanks for your help,' I say, walking away. 'I'm sure I'll find her.'

'014,' he says.

I turn round. 'What?'

'That's their apartment. 014. Ground floor.'

'What are you on about?' I ask, shaking my head. 'That's not their apartment. It's 110.'

'Just try it,' he says. He shakes his head as he pushes his door open and steps inside. 'I can't believe you didn't know about them changing their apartment. She's your friend, isn't she?' he adds before closing the door behind him.

Like everything else, his words make no sense to me, so I try not to dwell on them.

I decide to take the stairs now I'm at this end of the corridor. I might as well go home. They're bound to have left without me. The man obviously doesn't know what he's talking about. The Leonards always have this apartment – he must have been thinking of a different family

I check the car park on the way out. There's no sign of a gleaming sparkling Porsche, just a couple of old bangers that they wouldn't be seen dead in! I knew it. It's nearly twenty past two. They've gone without me.

But as I leave the car park, I glance at the ground floor apartments. They all open straight on to the path like ours do, but they're smaller than ours. Like everything else, they look different. The doors have changed colour! They used to be brown; now they're white. But that's impossible. They can't have painted them over-night, can they?

I glance at the number on the last one. 014. The one that man said was Autumn's apartment.

But he didn't know what he was on about, did he? He must have thought I was talking about someone else.

Still, there's nothing better to do, now I've missed Autumn, so I might as well give it a go.

I walk up to apartment 014 and take a deep breath. For some reason, a flutter of nerves twirl round in my stomach. *Don't be daft,* I say to myself. *What is there to be nervous about?*

Then I reach up, and knock on the door.

'Jenni. Am I pleased to see you!'

Autumn takes my hand and pulls me into the hallway.

At least, I *think* it's Autumn.

I mean, of course it's her, but she looks so different! Her hair that's always completely mad and full of life is lank and greasy. It's about six inches longer than it was this morning and hangs down the sides of her face like a damp mop.

Her eyes are black and ringed. She's wearing baggy jeans and a t-shirt that was possibly white at some point but is now a very unattractive grey – and I think it has a tea stain on it.

'Autumn?' I say tentatively. 'Are you . . . OK?'

She stops in the hallway. 'What d'you mean?'

'I – your – ' What can I say? *You look dreadful, and when was was the last time you washed you hair or your clothes?* I don't think so.

'Oh, you mean about being here?' she says.

57

Being here? *Being where?*

'Yeah, it's weird,' she goes on. 'It's really hard. To be honest I'm not sure why we've done it. Mum was insistent though. Last place we had a family holiday – she wanted to mark it, you know? Not that you could call it a holiday. More like torture. Come on, let's go in and sit down.'

As I follow Autumn into the living room of this strange apartment, I try to make sense of what she's just said – but fail badly. Out of all of it, the bit that almost puzzles me the most is the last bit. *Sit down?* When did Autumn ever voluntarily sit down?

We go into the living room and I follow Autumn to the sofas at the back of the room, looking around at this strange place.

Their normal apartment is one of the biggest of the whole complex. It's light and sunny with views for miles across the surrounding forest and hills; the windows are always open and they always have music on. Mrs Leonard likes world music with loads of drumming and Mr Leonard likes jazz. They always argue about what to put on – but there's always something.

This apartment is small, and still. The windows are closed. I'm struggling to breathe regularly. I don't know if it's because I'm starting to panic or because this place feels so closed and claustrophobic that there isn't enough oxygen for us both in here. And it's deathly quiet.

'Where is everyone?' I ask.

'Dad's at the pub – of course. Mum's not come out

of her room for about an hour. I think she's asleep,' she says.

'What about Mikey?'

Autumn shoots me a look of – what? Anger? Shock? Pain? All three of them, I think. She stares at me without speaking, till I feel my cheeks turn to balls of fire.

'What?' I ask.

'Jenni, that's not funny,' she says quietly.

'I wasn't trying to – ' I begin, but I stop myself. *Just don't say anything,* I tell myself. *Concentrate on trying to breathe and it'll make sense in a minute.*

'Do you want to watch a film?' Autumn asks, getting up to rifle through the collection of DVDs in a drawer by the telly. 'We'll need to stay in so we're here for when Mum gets up.'

Watch a film? Autumn never, and I mean *never,* suggests watching telly; not when there's a day to be explored and bounced around in. And anyway –

'Are we not going, then?' I ask.

'Going where?' Autumn says without turning round. She's reading the back of one of the DVDs. 'This looks good,' she says. 'Listen . . . '

'Horse riding,' I say.

Autumn drops the DVD on the floor and turns to look at me. Her face has turned a pale shade of grey; her eyes look like black wells, buried deep in a long, tired face. *'What?'* she says.

'Horse riding?' I repeat, more uncertainly this time. I can hear the quiver in my voice – what am I so scared of? What is *happening* here? 'You said two o' clock.'

Autumn slowly shakes her head. 'I can't believe you're saying this, Jenni.'

'I'm – I thought we were going horse riding,' I stammer, trying to hold on to the one thing I know for sure is meant to be happening. 'You persuaded me,' I continue. 'I didn't want to go but you insisted, and I knew it'd be fun – if I was there with you. So we were going. At two o'clock . . . ' My voice trails away and disappears into the silence of the living room, swallowed up and dying away to nothing.

Autumn rubs her eyes. 'I can't handle this. We've all been through enough. It wasn't an easy decision for us to come here, you know. Please don't make it worse with silly games.'

I haven't got the first idea what she's talking about. I haven't got the first clue what any of this is about. All I know is I'm starting to feel like I really can't breathe.

I stumble to my feet.

'Where are you going?' Autumn asks.

'I – I don't know,' I say. It seems to be my answer to everything right now – but I haven't got a better one.

'Jenni, I'm sorry,' Autumn says. 'Don't go. Come on, let's just hang out and try to be normal for a change. It's so long since we've spent proper time together.'

'What? We're always together!'

Autumn just gives me another of those looks, and I think she's about to answer, when a weak voice calls her name from one of the other rooms.

'Oh well, time's up I guess,' Autumn says, putting the DVD back in the drawer and getting up. 'Come on.'

I want to say 'Come on where?' but I don't even trust myself to speak any more, so I just follow her into the back bedroom.

The first thing I notice is how dark it is. The curtains are closed and there's a stale smell in the air. Not totally unpleasant, just not fresh and alive. And not how it normally smells when you're anywhere near Autumn's family. Apart from her mum's expensive perfume, their house always smells of paint or incense – and fresh air. Whatever the time of year, the windows are always open and the house always feels so *alive*.

It feels anything but alive now.

There's a suitcase on the floor which no one's bothered to unpack yet. The dark silence makes even the air feel heavy. There's a really horrible feeling crawling up through my body, which – like everything else in here – I can't explain.

Then I notice Autumn's mum.

She looks small and lost, sitting propped up on a chair in the corner. Her hair's loose and untidy. It often is, but this is different. It normally has that 'just got out of bed' look that takes hours to create. This time she clearly *has* just got out of bed. And she's wearing a baggy track suit. She never wears anything except either designer outfits or trendy jeans and paint-spattered smocks. Her eyes are dark.

'Mrs Leonard, I . . . ' *I what* exactly? *I think maybe I'm losing my mind and I wonder if you can help me find it?*

She turns her face in my direction and I notice there's a thin squiggly black line snaking down each cheek.

'Mrs Leonard! What's wrong?' I say.

'What's wrong?' she replies. 'What's wrong, Jenni?' Then she turns away again and doesn't say any more.

Then I realise – that's what must have happened. We're not going horse riding because Mrs Leonard is poorly and can't take us.

I turn to Autumn. 'You know, I could ask my mum if she could take us if you like?' I say. 'I don't think they'll have left for the candle museum yet.'

Autumn glares at me. 'What are you talking about, Jenni?'

Mrs Leonard drags a hand through her hair, or tries to, anyway. It snags on a knot. 'Take you where?' she asks.

'Nowhere,' Autumn says quickly. I open my mouth, but shut it again without saying anything.

In a lower voice, Autumn says, 'Jenni, please. You're going to upset Mum. I want to see if we can get her out of the bedroom today. Just think about what you're saying.'

I don't know *what* to think about what I'm saying, or what to think about what *she's* saying either. So I mutter 'OK,' and decide not to say anything else.

Autumn smiles at me. 'Thanks Jenni. You're such a good friend. I don't know how any of us would have coped this year without you.' Then, before I can even begin to ask what she means, she goes over to the window and starts to open the curtains. 'Right, come on now Mum,' she says in a bright tone of voice that sounds false – as though she's talking to a patient in a hospital, not the *naturally* bright voice she's always used for as long as I can remember. 'Let's get you up shall we?'

She pulls on the first curtain and her mum turns away. 'Close it,' she says firmly. 'Don't push me, Autumn; I'm not ready.'

Autumn drops the curtain and takes a sharp breath. 'OK,' she says calmly. 'Do you want a cup of tea, then?'

Mrs Leonard nods. 'Thank you,' she says in a whisper. 'You're good girls, both of you.'

I follow Autumn into the kitchen. This has gone far enough. I need to know what's going on.

'Autumn,' I say.

'Mm hm?' she says as she fills the kettle at the sink.

'Listen to me.'

'I'm listening.'

'Autumn, look at me,' I say.

Autumn flicks the kettle on and turns round. 'What?' she says, turning round to look at me. Her face is so pale, her eyes so tired and big and – sad.

'Autumn, what's happened?' I ask.

'What d'you mean?'

'I mean everything! Your mum, you, even the apartment. It's all different!'

Autumn looks round the apartment. 'I know,' she says. 'Pretty awful, isn't it? It's the best we can do at the moment, now we've not got the income any more. I didn't want to come at all, but Mum and Dad thought it would help, you know, come to terms with it.'

'Autumn – stop!' I shout, slamming my hands over my ears. I can't listen to this any longer. I can't cope with hearing all these things that don't make sense any more.

Autumn takes a step towards me. 'Jenni, what is it?' she asks, her voice full of concern. 'Are you OK? Has something happened to you?'

I shake my head. 'Has something happened to *me*?' I say numbly. I don't know what else to say. I take a big breath and let it out in a long whistle as I try to find the words.

'Autumn – my head is bursting with so many questions I think it's going to explode.'

'What questions? Tell me. You can still tell me everything, you know. You don't need to stop yourself just because of all this. I'm still your best friend.'

I nod. OK. Questions. Where to start?

'Where's your dad?' I ask eventually.

Autumn laughs drily. 'Like I said, at the pub, I presume,' she says. 'Where else would he be?'

Her answer makes about as much sense as everything else. Autumn's parents are hardly ever apart, and they don't generally drink anything except champagne or cocktails. Mr Leonard certainly isn't the type to hang out in his local pub.

'So where's Mikey?' I ask.

Autumn's jaw falls open. 'Why are you asking me that?' she says.

I stare back at her. 'I just thought ... he – he's not here. Is he in his room?'

Autumn stares harder at me; her eyes fill with tears. 'Autumn, what's the matter?' I ask. 'What's happened?

Has something happened to Mikey since this morning?'

'Since this *morning*?'

'Well – at all, then?'

Autumn rubs the back of her hand across her eyes and wipes her sleeve against her nose. 'You really want me to spell out where Mikey is?' she asks.

I nod, biting hard on my lip. I don't trust myself to speak.

'Jenni, Mikey is where he's been for the last year.'

For the last year? But he was with them yesterday. I saw him! I don't say anything; I just wait for her to continue.

'He's at the hospital.'

I clutch my throat. I think I'm going to be sick. 'Why?' I eventually manage to squeeze out.

Autumn shakes her head again. 'This is unbelievable, Jenni. *Why*? Where else do you expect him to be?'

'I – I don't know. I don't know why he's in a hospital. What's the matter with him?'

'What's the matter? Jenni, I don't know what you're playing at here, but if you need me to spell it out for you I will. Mikey's in exactly the same place he's been for a year. Back at home. In a hospital bed. In a coma.'

'Jenni, are you all right?' Autumn's leaning over me, waving a bottle of something strong-smelling over my face. I cough and sit up.

'What happened?' I ask.

'I think you might have fainted,' Autumn says. 'D'you want to try to get up?'

I sit up and look at her. I try to take everything in, and fail miserably.

Autumn helps me up and I go over to sit on the sofa. She gets a glass of water and sits down next to me. 'Drink this,' she says. 'You'll feel better.'

When did she get to be so thoughtful? The Autumn I thought I knew would have slapped me on my arm, told me to pull myself together and dragged me out on some adventure. She wouldn't be fetching me glasses of water and looking at me with concern.

'Thanks,' I say, taking a long drink and letting the cool water slip down my throat. 'I feel a bit better now.'

She smiles at me – but the smile doesn't reach her dark eyes. They look as though they've got an invisible veil inside them and she's hidden behind it. It's as if what makes her Autumn has slipped out of her.

She points at my neck. 'Hey, nice to see you dug that out.' I reach up and touch the friendship necklace that she gave me only this morning. 'Look, let's forget what happened before, shall we? Start again. Tell me what you've been up to since I last saw you. It's been ages!'

I laugh. 'Ages?'

Autumn half smiles, a tiny hint of the old Autumn shining behind her eyes. 'Well, at least two days. Ages for you and me.'

I rest my forehead heavily on my palm. I need something to steady me. 'I saw you – ' I look at my watch. Twenty to three. 'I saw you a couple of hours ago,'

I say, virtually choking on my words. They feel like bricks coming out of my mouth. 'We were going horse riding,' I add in a dull monotone. 'You said don't be late.'

Autumn takes a sharp breath. 'Not this again.' She leans forward and puts a hand out to touch my arm. 'Look, Jenni, I don't know what's going on here. You're not playing some kind of trick are you?'

It's the second time today I've been accused of that. 'Do I look like I'm playing a trick, Autumn?' Then it suddenly hits me. Maybe that's what *she's* doing. For the second time today, I latch on to the possibility that this is all one big prank. A terrible, awful, really sick joke. I can hardly believe Autumn would try to pull off something so horrible – but suddenly it's the only solution that makes sense. Autumn loves practical jokes. That *must* be what it is.

'Autumn, are you messing about? Are you having a laugh with me?' I ask.

Autumn just looks at me. 'A laugh, Jenni?' She gets up and takes my glass into the kitchen. 'I'm going to pretend you didn't say that,' she says without turning round.

I get up and follow her into the kitchen. I grab her arms. 'Autumn,' I say. 'This is awful. I can't bear it.' Then I stop. My head drops into my hands.

She puts the glass down. 'What is it?' she asks gently. 'What's happened? What's going on Jen? Is it something at home?'

I shake my head. Better not to try speaking. Any

minute now, my words are going to swallow me up, turn me inside out. Maybe I'll disappear, the floor sliding open and I'll gradually fall away, slip into nothingness. Like my life has done.

I take a deep breath, blowing the air back out through my palms. 'Autumn, something really strange has happened.'

'What?'

'The last time I saw you . . . '

'The day before yesterday?'

I close my eyes. 'This morning.'

'I didn't *see* you this morning.'

'Yes you did! Look. Just hear me out OK?'

'OK,' Autumn agrees with a shrug.

I take a breath. 'The last time I saw you, it was just before lunch,' I say, choosing my words carefully. 'We were going horse riding.' Autumn opens her mouth to speak and I carry on quickly before she interrupts me. 'You said don't be late. But I *was* late. I couldn't find you. You weren't at the apartment. A man told me to come here. And I did. And now I'm here, and nothing makes sense.' I look at Autumn. She's staring blankly at me, as though her face is a mask with nothing behind it. My voice is rising, growing tight and sharp as I try to hold myself together. 'I don't know what's happening to me.' A tear slips out of my eye and runs down my cheek. 'I think maybe I'm going crazy.'

Autumn takes a step closer and puts her arms round me. 'Hey, come on now, it's all right,' she says. 'It's all OK, we'll work it out.'

'How can we work it out?' I wail, tears running freely down my face now. 'You don't understand. I've lost my mind. How can anything be all right?'

I can't speak any more. Autumn holds me tight and I sob on her shoulder.

Eventually, the sobbing calms down. Autumn's shoulder is wet from my tears. I move away. 'Sorry.'

'Hey, I'm used to it round here,' she says with a wry smile.

'Look, can I use the bathroom?' I ask. 'I need to wash my face.'

'Course.' Autumn points down the corridor. 'Last door on the left.'

In the bathroom, I grab some toilet roll and blow my nose. Then I sit down on the side of the bath to gather my thoughts. But I can't. They're too tangled and mangled and they don't match up with each other, like a drawer full of odd socks.

I get up and run the tap. Nice and cold. Cupping my hands under the water, I glance up at my face.

Horror fills me.

I grab the sink, splashing water all down my front. *It can't be.*

In the mirror, I watch my fingers reach up to touch my face. It's me. But it's not me. Not the me I thought I was. I'm wearing the same clothes. My new blue t-shirt with 'Gorgeous' written across it. My khaki shorts. My clothes that I suddenly realise feel tighter than usual. With everything else that's been going on, I hadn't even noticed that. And my hair – what's happened to

it? It's all gone! Too short to be tied back. I hadn't realised. Why would I? Why didn't Autumn mention it?

I grab at my hair. My fingers run easily through the
short curls. I feel the back. The hair's smooth and thin,
tickling the back of my neck in wisps.

'You OK in there, Jen?' Autumn calls through the
door.

I try to reply. Nothing comes out. I can't tear my
eyes away from my face.

'Jen? Are you all right?'

I make a kind of choking noise. It's all I can manage.

'Jenni, I'm coming in, OK?'

As she opens the door, I tear my eyes away from the
mirror to look at her. I'm pointing at it. At the glass;
the lying, tricking glass. At the face streaked with tears.

The face that is undeniably a year older than it was
this morning.

6

'What's wrong, Jenni? What's happened?'

'What's happened?' I gasp. 'Look!' I stab my finger at the mirror.

Autumn looks at the mirror. 'What's wrong with it?'

'Not the *mirror*!' I scream. 'Me! Look at *me*!'

Autumn takes my hand and talks in that calm manner which she suddenly seems to have developed today and which I've never in my life heard her use before. 'Come back into the living room, Jenni. I'll make you a cup of camomile tea.'

'I don't want camomile tea!' I yell as the panic surges through my body. 'I want to know what's happened to me!'

'Let's just sit down and we can work out what's going on. It can't be easy for you. It's my fault, I've relied on you too much. It's all got to you. Come on, I'll—'

'Have you got another mirror?'

'Another – well, yeah. There's one in my bedroom, second door on the right.'

'Let me see,' I say. I get half way down the corridor.

But what's the point? I don't need another mirror. My hands can't be lying to me, running through the short crop of hair on my head. My eyes aren't imagining all of this. It's not just me; it's Autumn, and her mum, the apartment. It's everything.

Autumn's following me to her room. 'Go on; have a look in my room if you like.'

'It doesn't matter,' I say flatly.

We go back into the living room and I flop back on to the sofa.

'Are you all right?' Autumn asks, reaching out a hand to me.

I don't reply. I can't.

'You'll be OK,' she goes on. 'I'm not going to rely on you so much any more. The stress has got to you.'

'What stress?' I mumble.

'All of the last year. You've done so much, helping me look after Mum and Dad, helping us all cope with everything, coming to see Mikey with me – none of it's been easy.'

I wince at the mention of Mikey's name. Little Mikey in a coma? It's not possible. I saw him yesterday! And now he's gone. Invisible, like his dad.

Wait.

Invisible. Autumn's joke this morning.

'Autumn.' I grab the arm of the chair. 'Do you remember making that joke about becoming invisible?'

'What joke?'

'Just before. Just – I don't know. When we couldn't find each other. You said maybe you'd become invisible. And we were talking about parallel lives and stuff. Don't you remember?'

Autumn frowns. 'Vaguely. I think. But that was ages ago! That was last year, Jenni!'

'It wasn't! It was this morning!'

Autumn takes another of those long breaths. 'Jenni, let me look at your head,' she says. 'I think you might have concussion.'

I let her examine me. 'Does it hurt?' she asks gently.

'I didn't bang my head,' I say calmly. 'I'm not concussed. Why won't you believe me?'

'How can I?' Autumn says. 'You're not making any sense!'

I shake my head. She's right. 'No, I'm not. Sorry. Maybe I knocked myself out or something. Maybe I'm dreaming.'

'Look,' she says, getting up. 'Why don't we go for a walk?'

'But what about your mum?'

'She'll be OK for a bit. Come on, we need some fresh air.'

She's right. I need to get out of this apartment.

Autumn pokes her head into her mum's room, then closes the door behind her and softly pads back up the corridor. 'She's gone back to bed,' she says. 'We'll be fine for half an hour or so.'

'Right. Let's get out of here.'

We walk along the path, down to our place by the river. For a second, it almost feels like normal. Just Autumn and me walking along together, hanging out. And it would be fine if I could somehow walk without seeing anything around me. But everywhere, I see signs of change. Nothing major – nothing that makes much sense when you say it out loud – but just enough to completely disorientate me and remind me that my world has spun off to somewhere that I don't recognise. Little things, like the car park. There's a fence round it, and each space is marked out and labelled with an apartment number. It wasn't like that an hour ago.

And I'm *sure* the trees at the end of Autumn's row are taller. They were little sprigs this morning. And there's a brand new building behind Autumn's block. I'm sure it never used to be there. And the ivy on the reception building – it looks bushier.

Am I imagining it? Has everything changed? It *can't* have done. But if not, then how can I walk around here every year and not even properly see what's around me?

'When did they do that?' I ask, pointing at the fence in the car park.

Autumn shrugs. 'Some time this year, I guess. It was like that when we got here.'

'Where's your car? Don't tell me your dad's gone out in it – not if he's drinking.'

Autumn scans the car park and points to an old Fiesta in the corner. 'It's there!' she says.

I swallow hard. It's the final straw. Autumn's dad drove here in a battered old Fiesta?

'That's not your car,' I say, but without any conviction. If everything else has changed, why should this be any different?

'Er, I think it is,' Autumn says.

'But the Porsche – ' I say, the words almost catching in my throat, 'Your dad loves that car.' I try to latch on to one last thread of hope, desperate to find normality somewhere – anywhere! 'Did something happen this morning? Is it being serviced or something?'

Autumn lets out a deep breath. 'Are you *trying* to upset me, Jenni?' she asks quietly, walking ahead and not turning to look at me. 'Because you're going the right way about it.'

I run to catch her up. We've reached the bridge over the river and stand leaning on the railing. 'I'm not trying to upset you! I promise. I just—'

Autumn turns and stares at me. 'Jenni, he sold it,' she says. 'You were with me the day they took it. Do you honestly not remember?'

I shake my head, my mouth clamped shut. I daren't speak. I hardly dare breathe.

'Jen, I think something serious has happened to you,' she says. At last.

'I know. Something really bad has happened. I just don't know what it is.'

'I think you've got amnesia. You know, we've talked to lots of doctors this year and they've told us about all the different coping mechanisms. Maybe this is yours?'

I bite away the tears that I can feel welling up and burning the back of my eyes. 'Autumn, what happened with the car?' I ask. 'Maybe if you tell me, it'll bring a memory back.'

Autumn leans back down on the railing, staring at the river as it trickles and bubbles obliviously along below us. She turns back to me. 'You promise you don't remember?' she asks again.

'I promise. Tell me what happened.'

'It was one of the worst weeks,' she begins, then she laughs. A dry, cracked laugh with no humour in it. 'Although there've been plenty to choose from. On the Monday, Mum got the letter from the gallery saying she'd been fired.'

'Why?'

'She'd been taking too many days off to go to the hospital. She spent virtually the whole of the first six months in there. They were pretty understanding at first, but then they said they couldn't afford to keep paying her wages and pay another person to come in and cover her job, too. So they thanked her for all her years of work, gave her another six months' pay and told her they were letting her go.'

'Just like that?'

'Just like that. She built that place from nothing.'

'I know.' Autumn's parents were very proud of their story. She was brought in to run a tiny, struggling art gallery, and she built it into a major exhibition centre, selling famous works from around the world – including Autumn's dad's. 'What about your dad's work?'

'That was Tuesday's news. His next exhibition got cancelled. At least that one wasn't a surprise. He hadn't painted a thing all year, so how he was meant to hand over twenty new works? We all knew it was going to happen.'

'I don't know what to say,' I say, feeling helpless, useless.

'And then on Wednesday, we sold the car and the fancy timeshare here. Three days; one big demolition job on our lives.'

I lean forward on my elbows and cover my face with my hands. *Where was I when all this happened? Why can't I remember?*

'It was only last month that we decided to get this apartment. I didn't want to come back. Dad probably doesn't care one way or another *where* we are as long as there's a pub nearby. But Mum – she thought it would be good for us.'

'Do you think she was right?' I ask.

Autumn does that dry laugh again. 'Look at us, Jen. My best friend has developed amnesia; Mum's shut away in her bedroom and Dad's done his invisibility act as usual. How good does that sound to you?'

Invisible. That word again. It's how I feel. As though that's what I've been for a year. The world has passed me by and somehow I wasn't there. I don't like it.

'Autumn, let's move on,' I say. I need to keep moving. I need to stop myself from staying still and focusing on what's going on. Keep moving, keep doing and don't think too much.

As we get closer to our place, I notice that the families who were here earlier have gone. We walk over the last bit of rough track to the bushes. Yesterday, you had to pick your way across them, virtually climbing over branches to get to our spot, but now the river is so shallow there's enough bay to walk round.

I rummage through the pebbles, looking for a flat one. I find one and hand it to Autumn.

She smiles sadly. 'I'd forgotten about skimming stones,' she says. She goes over to the water's edge and throws it perfectly across the river. It bounces five times.

I pick one up and throw it across the water. It trips over the surface once before flumping into the lake with a plop.

'You're still the stone skimming champion of the world,' I say.

Autumn smiles again. This time it almost seems to reach her eyes and for a split second, things feel normal. Then she turns to me. 'Jenni, what are we going to do about this?' she asks.

I bend down and rummage through the stones, looking for some more flat ones. 'I don't know. I'm scared.'

'What of?'

'Look, I don't think it's amnesia,' I say. 'It's not me. I don't feel any different. It's everything around me that's changed. I feel exactly the same.'

'But that's exactly how it is with amnesia!'

'I know,' I say, frustration biting at my throat. 'But it doesn't *feel* like amnesia. It doesn't feel like I've lost my memory. It's – I don't know. It's too weird.'

'What d'you mean?'

'I don't know. Just – it's not as if I've forgotten things. It's as if it's all changed, in a split second. Everything's different from how it was this morning. Except it wasn't this morning. It was a year ago.'

Autumn just stares at me.

'I know what you're thinking,' I say.

'What am I thinking?'

'That I'm describing amnesia.'

Autumn doesn't say anything, but her look says it all.

I sit down on the pebbles. 'A whole year,' I say quietly. 'and I don't remember it.'

Autumn sits down beside me. 'Look, what's the last thing you *do* remember?' she asks.

'You coming round to our apartment,' I say woodenly. 'We were going horse riding.' My eyes fill with tears as I hang on to this simple, useless fact. 'You said don't be late.'

'And that's it? That's really the last thing you remember?'

I nod.

'Jen, you swear you're not having me on?'

'Of course I'm not!'

Autumn breathes a low whistle out through her teeth. 'Wow.'

We stare at the river in silence. The water glides past, smooth swells running into tiny whirlpools around the bigger rocks.

'It must have been when you fell,' she says after a

while. 'You must have hit your head. We just didn't realise how bad it was.'

'But I'd forgotten stuff before that. I didn't know you were in that apartment.'

'Maybe you fainted before that, too.'

'I don't make a habit of just falling down all over the place, you know,' I say. 'Anyway, I'd have remembered if I'd done that.'

Autumn just looks at me.

'OK, maybe I wouldn't have remembered. But it all feels so weird. I can remember this morning so clearly.'

'But it *wasn't* this morning,' Autumn insists.

'See, even you,' I say.

'Even me what?'

I pause. I don't want to hurt her feelings. 'You've changed,' I say carefully.

'How?'

'You don't believe me. You're looking for rational explanations.'

'Well, of course I am. What – you want me to say you've been abducted by aliens or something?'

'The old Autumn would have said exactly that!'

'Well the old Autumn didn't know anything about reality,' she says flatly. 'The old Autumn was quite happy living in a childish make-believe world where bad things didn't happen and where you could make up whatever silly story you liked and tell yourself it was true.'

'And the new Autumn?'

Autumn stands up and brushes stones and gravel from her legs. 'The new Autumn knows that the world isn't like that,' she says. 'Come on, we should be getting back. I don't want Mum to wake up in an empty apartment.'

We head back to the apartment blocks in silence. My thoughts all seem to be buried under mush and I don't know how to articulate a single one.

We get to Autumn's block. I know I should offer to go in with her, but I can't face going back in there.

'Listen, I'd better go in on my own, OK? Spend a bit of time with Mum,' Autumn says, as if she's read my mind. Or maybe she just doesn't want me around. I wouldn't be surprised. The last thing she needs right now is a best friend who's only adding to her problems.

'See you later?' I ask.

Autumn nods. Her face is empty and lifeless. It's like a mask made from grey cardboard. It's like someone else. Not Autumn. This isn't Autumn.

As she walks up the path to her apartment, I'm desperate for her to turn round, flash me one of her brilliant grins and tell me it's all a big mistake. Her biggest, cleverest, most horrible practical joke.

A tiny part of my brain is still clinging to the hope that she'll get to the door, then turn and scream, 'Sucker!'

She doesn't. She goes into the apartment and closes the door behind her without turning round to wave.

Now what? I'm stuck in this strange world that I don't recognise, and the one person in the world I'd normally want to share it all with – the one who would usually help me make sense of it, figure it all out with me as though it's a big exciting adventure – she's gone, and I'm standing out on a path on my own.

Which is when it occurs to me: if she's right about it being amnesia because of the shock and everything to do with Mikey, perhaps it's only all the things to do with *her* family that I've forgotten. Perhaps everything will be completely normal with *my* family. Maybe I'll remember everything as soon as I get back to my parents, and to Craig. And then once I've remembered everything with them, I'll remember everything to do with Autumn too.

The idea makes more sense than anything else that's happened, and I find myself practically running back to our apartment, excited and relieved that I've got a plan for how to get out of this nightmare.

My legs are like jelly as I stand outside our door.

I reach for the handle, my hand shaking, and push the door open. I waver, my hand gripping the handle so tightly my fingers turn white.

What if I'm wrong? What if I *never* remember the last year and I'm lost in this confusion forever? What if it's not amnesia, and it's something that I'll never be able to understand or explain to anyone?

What am I going to find in here?

I could turn back now. No one's heard me. I could go. Run away. Go to sleep or something. Maybe if I do that, my memory will be back when I wake up. Maybe this is all a dream! That's why none of it makes sense. It's not even happening!

But I know I'm kidding myself. I'm not dreaming. However crazy and frightening it is, whatever's happening here is real. I have to get to the bottom of it – and whether it gives me all the answers or not, I have to face whatever might be waiting for me in our apartment.

I step inside and close the door behind me.

The hallway is filled with junk. That's the first thing. Coats on the floor, shoes everywhere. And a buggy. I stare at it with the same level of amazement as I would if it had just dropped out of a flying saucer in the sky.

And then I go into the living room.

The difference there is almost as shocking as anything I've seen so far. If you knew my parents, you'd understand what I mean.

The apartment that's always so ordered, so neat and tidy, with nothing ever out of place, is *littered* with clothes, toys, blankets, scrunched-up tissues, dirty plates, half-drunk drinks, plastic bottles, congealed food on plates around the dining room table, unwashed dishes filling up the sink.

This is not my family's apartment. It is absolutely 100% the wrong place. I've walked into the wrong apartment – simple as that. It's the only explanation.

I'm about to turn round and walk straight out – when someone speaks.

'Jenni, thank goodness you're here,' Dad's voice says. I wonder if that's how *everyone* greets each other in this strange new world. I also wonder why the furniture spoke to me with Dad's voice.

And then his head pops up from behind the sofa. 'Give us a hand will you?' he says. 'Your mum'll be here any minute. She'll kill us if it's like this when she gets back. You know what she's like.'

Do I? I'm not sure I know what anyone's like. I don't think I know anything about *anything* any more.

Dad grabs a bowl of congealed goo from the floor in front of the sofa, picks up a few tiny items of clothing from the floor and nudges me on his way past. 'Jenni, come on; shape up, love. She'll be back any minute.'

I want to ask so many things. I want to ask who all these tiny clothes belong to, since the last time I looked, any baby in this family was still firmly inside Mum's stomach and not going anywhere for at least another month. But then if I really do have amnesia, I suppose things have moved on from then.

I want to ask if we've been ransacked and burgled since I went out – but I don't want to offend – just in case we haven't.

And I want to ask where Craig is – but after what's happened to Mikey, that question turns into a hard knot of iron and gets stuck in my throat.

So I do the only thing I can do: I get started on the washing up.

'Thanks love, you're a star,' Dad says, bringing more plates and bowls with congealed mess in them to the sink and giving me a kiss on my shoulder. 'Let's get this place as straight as we can. I don't think I could cope with another of your mum's meltdowns today – you know what I mean?'

'Mm,' I say. No I don't know what he means. Mum's meltdowns? Mum and Dad don't do meltdowns. They talk reasonably and calmly and they work everything out efficiently and sensibly.

I'm still trying to figure out what Dad could have meant by this when a blood-curdling scream fills the air. I leap about a foot in the air and drop three plates in the sink in the process, splashing soapy water all over my t-shirt.

'What on earth was—' I begin.

'Blast – will you get her, love?' Dad says as he wipes the dining room table. 'She'll probably need changing.'

I turn to stare at my dad. I have soapy water all down my front, I have a best friend whose life is in tatters because the most awful thing – which I have no recollection of at all – has happened to her brother, and now I am being asked, perfectly casually, to 'change' someone I have no idea exists. How on earth am I meant to respond to that?

'Sure, Dad,' I say with a smile, and head upstairs in the direction of the howling, which has now increased to a glass-splitting siren wail.

I check the door to the bedroom I share with Craig. The sight of Dirty Boy's jeans and piles of cars and diggers scattered everywhere makes me sigh with relief. At least some things haven't changed.

The sound is coming from Mum and Dad's room.

My heart is pounding ridiculously heavily in my chest as I gently turn the handle and go in. There's a cot in the far corner, mangled sheets hanging over the side and a teddy lying face down on the bedroom floor next to it.

I pick up the teddy and put him back in the cot. As I do, the source of the screaming – a tiny, red-faced, wet-cheeked image of Craig when he was a baby – turns its bright blue eyes on me, and breaks into a smile that feels like the sun coming out from behind the heaviest cloud in the sky. The pink babygrow with a fairy on it confirms that Mum was wrong about it being a boy.

I smile back, instantly in love with this little person who I presume is my sister. 'Hello, you,' I say, lifting what is admittedly a very smelly baby out of the warm cot, and clearing my throat to get beyond the emotion croaking into my voice.

I think of all the times that Mum's called me and Craig her little angels. She always wanted three of us, though. She reckons that's the perfect family. She says that's why cars have two seats in the front and three in the back. That's what it should be, that's nature's way. I always found myself wondering whether car designs and nature have really got that much to do with each other, but I knew there'd be no point in saying any-thing. When Mum gets something into her head, she can find a million signs that prove she's right.

And now she's got her third little angel.

The baby gurgles and dribbles onto her chin. I lean

forward to kiss her head, breathing in her soft scent as I do.

'You're without doubt the best thing that's happened to me today,' I whisper into the fluffy wisps of blonde hair scattered on her little head.

Clutching her tightly, I fish around in the bag next to her cot for a nappy. Then I lay her down on the bed, tickling her and making her giggle as I remove the cause of the pong, clean her up and put a fresh nappy on her. I used to do this all the time with Craig. I was only about seven when I first did it but it was just like this. He'd stare at me and giggle all the way through nappy-changing time, then reach out for me to lift him up afterwards, just like my brand new little sister is doing now.

I hold her close and kiss her plump little cheeks, blowing raspberries on her face to make her giggle even more, and we head downstairs together.

Dad's somehow managed to transform the living room while I've been gone. It looks much more like the Green family household again now. Nothing strewn across the floor. No dirty dishes anywhere. Calm restored.

'Hello my little pumpkin pie,' Dad says to the baby whose name I've suddenly realised I don't even know. It's not exactly the kind of thing I can ask, either. *Er, s'cuse me Dad, what's my little sister called again? Only, I've momentarily forgotten; you know how it is.* No I don't think so. I guess I'll have to call her Pumpkin Pie for now as well.

She reaches her little arms out for Dad and he takes her from me and kisses her neck with big squishy kisses that make her giggle so much she hiccoughs.

I smile as I watch them, and for the first time since this nightmare started, I'm almost happy to be here.

Then Dad says something that reminds me why I could never, ever be happy in this new reality.

'How were Autumn and her parents? They doing OK?'

Once again I have no idea how to answer this. *Oh yeah, you know – Dad's drunk, Mum's like a zombie, Autumn's like a ghost of her former self and Mikey's in a coma back at home. They're fine!*

Luckily, I don't get the chance to reply, as the front door is thrown open and there's a bustling noise in the hallway.

'Phew, just in time, eh?' Dad says to me with a wink. 'Now don't upset your mum, OK?'

Upset my mum? Why would I do that?

'We're home!' The front door slams and Craig bursts through the door. An elongated version of little Craig. He's shot up. He must be a full hand taller than when I last saw him – two hours ago! His face has thinned out, and he's got two big front teeth where he used to have a gap.

'Guess what?' he says, bursting into the room. 'Mum was talking to the new man and he said we can go on the train in the front carriage and I can help drive it 'cos he knows the driver and he said he'll talk to him specially for us.'

He plonks himself down two centimetres away from the telly and switches it on.

'Hi, love,' Mum says to me as she follows Craig into the living room and automatically turns the TV down. Her face is tired, and more serious than usual. Her hair is tied up in a neat bun – and she looks like a rake compared to this morning. Well, this morning she was eight months pregnant!

It's only when she goes over to Dad and takes Pumpkin Pie off him that she looks anything like her old self again. It's as though looking at the baby switches on a light behind Mum's eyes.

'Did you have a nice time, darling?' Dad asks gently.

Mum's busy rearranging the baby's clothes. I must have put her trousers back on wrong when I changed her nappy. 'Lovely,' she says with a quick smile. 'Have you changed her?'

'I did it,' I said.

Mum turns to Dad. 'Did you remember to put the sides up when you put her to bed?'

'Yep,' Dad says.

'All the way?'

Dad's voice tightens a touch. 'Yes darling, all the way,' he says.

Mum nods. 'Right, who wants some juice?' she asks, jogging the baby on her hip as she goes into the kitchen. At the sink, she spins round, the baby on her hip, obliviously twirling mum's hair round her tiny fingers. 'Tom, what's this?' she asks, pointing at the washing up that's draining next to the sink.

Dad joins her in the kitchen. 'Er . . . '

She hands him the baby and starts gathering things up from the drainer. 'Knives, Tom? You left *knives* lying about?'

'I've only just finished washing up,' Dad says, still calm, but an edge of exasperation creeping into his voice. 'They were on the surfaces before. At least they're clean now.'

'Oh, my mistake. You left *clean* knives lying around, and they're on the drainer, rather than the surfaces! Well, that's much better isn't it? You do know that 80 per cent of household accidents occur in the kitchen don't you?'

'Yes dear,' Dad says. More quietly, he adds, 'You've only told me about a hundred times.'

Mum just shakes her head as she noisily puts all the knives away. Then she surveys the room, as though checking it for any more potentially life-threatening hazards. Clearly satisfied that there aren't any, she goes back to the fridge and gets the juice out.

'Do you want one?' she asks without looking at either of us.

I look at Dad, and realise for the first time that he looks different, too. Not as different as everyone else, but different nevertheless. More tired. And there are a few spots of grey in his dark hair which I'm sure weren't there this morning. But, who knows, this morning's already feeling like a lifetime ago.

'What's up with her?' I mouth at him.

Dad pulls a *'Just leave it'* face at me before handing

me the baby and going to join Mum in the kitchen. He gets two cups out of the cupboard, gives her a tiny kiss on her cheek, and smiles gently at her, as though she's an old lady he's helping across the road. 'I booked a table,' he says.

Mum looks vacantly at him. 'Table?'

'For tonight; our anniversary.'

'Oh yes. That. OK. As long as Jenni's sure about Thea.'

Thea? I look at the baby. *Is that you?* 'Course I am,' I say, more than happy to spend the evening with my little sister.

Mum glances across at us. 'I don't know,' she says to Dad. 'Can we see how she is later?'

'Jenni will be fine with Thea, and so will Craig, won't you Craig?'

Craig grunts a reply without looking away from the telly.

Dad puts his arms round Mum's waist. 'Darling, they'll be fine. Nothing's going to happen to anyone. We can call them every half an hour just to check. But it's our sixteen-year anniversary and I would like to take my wife out to celebrate. OK?'

Mum looks at him, and finally smiles. 'OK,' she says. Then she gives him a quick peck on the cheek and wriggles out of his arms so she can make the drinks.

Dad comes back into the living room and we sit down on the sofa together.

'What's *up* with her?' I ask in a whisper.

'What d'you mean?'

'Why's she being like this? Mum's never moody.'

Dad runs a hand through his hair. 'What planet are you living on, Jenni? Have you actually been around for the last year?'

'Good question,' I say under my breath.

'What?'

I shake my head. 'Nothing.'

'You know how all the stuff with Mikey's affected her,' Dad goes on. 'She just needs a bit of time to get back to normal.'

Hmm. Don't we all? I kiss Thea on her soft little head and hold her out to Dad. 'I'm going out, OK?'

'Do you have to? You only just got back in,' he says, taking Thea and cuddling her.

I look round at the room, at all of them, and suddenly I can't take it – any of it. 'Yes, I do have to,' I say.

'Can I come?' Craig asks instantly, breaking away from the telly for the first time since he came in.

'No.' I need to be on my own. I've got too many questions racing round in my head to start dealing with Craig.

'Be back in an hour at the latest, all right?' Dad calls. 'I'd like to spend a little time all together before we go for our meal.'

'No problem,' I say, and I make my escape.

My head's spinning as I walk aimlessly along the path. I keep looking for things that have changed. I'm sure there's a tree missing – and wasn't that blue shed green this morning? Everything's so familiar, and yet so different. It's too spooky.

I automatically head over to Autumn's block. But

I stop outside her new apartment. No, I can't do it. I can't go back to see her. That would be even worse than our apartment.

I need something that makes sense to me. Something that can help me work out where my life has gone. But there's nothing that can do that, and nowhere I can go. I'm totally alone, and lost in a strange world that isn't my life.

Wait!

Who said that? Someone said almost exactly the same thing – I'm sure of it.

With a shiver that snakes the length of my body, from my head to my toes and back up again, I remember who it was. The woman upstairs, in Autumn's old apartment. I remember her words exactly because they were so strange.

No one knows; no one ever knew. Only me. Always lost.

That's exactly how I feel!

Does she . . . could she . . . Is it possible that she might know something?

One thing's for sure – I'm not going to get answers anywhere else. If there's a chance she could help, I've got to try asking her.

And before I can talk myself out of it, I'm inside the building and taking the lift up to Autumn's old apartment. The normal lift, that is. The old one is closed and silent beside it.

'I only want a minute of your time,' I say quickly, before the woman's had a chance to tell me to go away.

She's holding on to the door, almost hidden behind it, her face peering round the side.

'I've got to understand something,' I say. 'I need your help.'

'Why?' she asks suspiciously. 'How on earth could I help you? You've come to make fun of me again, haven't you?'

'No! I haven't. I promise.' I can see she's about to close the door in my face – and part of me thinks I might as well give up. But then another part – a new part, a part of me I don't even recognise – speaks up firmly. 'Don't shut the door on me. Please. I need someone I can talk to.'

She looks at me for a long time, searching my face, her eyes screwed up tight, as though scanning me with a lie detector.

'Very well,' she says eventually. Opening her door, she adds, 'You can have five minutes.'

I follow her into the apartment. 'I'd offer you a drink but I've only got rose hip tea and you won't want that.'

'I'm fine, thanks.' I wave away her offer, if that's what it was.

She sits down at the table and points to a chair opposite her. 'Now, what can I do for you?' she asks, flattening down her dress in her lap.

'I don't really know,' I say.

'Well that's a fine start, isn't it?'

'I just – it's just that I came here, and then everything changed.'

'Everything changed? Now she's not even making sense,' the woman says to the room, as though there was an audience sitting on the sofa.

'I came up here. Where Autumn comes each year.'

'Autumn again. Now I've told—'

'Where she used to come,' I continue quickly. 'She's my friend. Or she was. Well, she still is, but – anyway, I was coming up here to see her.'

'Now listen – what's your name? And please don't say something ridiculous like Spring or Sunshine.' She purses her lips together in a tight frown. I wish she didn't seem so cross, but then I imagine having some girl turn up at your door for the third time talking absolute drivel isn't strictly the best way to bring patience and kindness out in people.

'Jenni,' I say. 'With an I.'

She raises an eyebrow. 'Right. Well, Jenni with an I, I'm Mrs Smith. With an I, too, as it happens. Not very original I know. Not my fault I'm afraid.' Then she smiles a touch.

'It's OK,' I say, feeling more stupid every time I open my mouth.

'So tell me, Jenni,' Mrs Smith continues over me. 'Why were you so convinced you'd find your friend here?'

'This is where they've always had their apartment. I only saw her this morning. She said it was definitely here. I made her tell me the number again just to be sure.'

Mrs Smith stares at me for a long time. I stare back. As I do, it's as if I can see past the front she's putting on, right behind it to the woman I met the first time I came here. The kindly, helpful, nice lady – the one who hadn't had some girl show up three times with stories that don't make sense.

'I'm sorry,' I say, wanting to make it better for her. Why should she get dragged into my crazy mess? 'Look, I got it wrong. I know I did. I just don't understand how, or why I'm the only person out of step with things that everyone else is taking for granted.'

Mrs Smith doesn't say anything. She just keeps staring at me. I feel as if she can see right inside me, all the way into my soul. Can you see the truth in there? *Can you tell me what's happened?*

'Yes dear,' she says, her voice soft like it was the first time. 'You just got it wrong. Everyone makes mistakes.'

'But I didn't make a – ' I begin, and then I stop. What's the point? I don't want to annoy her again.

'They must have changed apartments,' she goes on. 'Your friend is obviously as confused as you are! This is only my first year here.' She pauses, her eyelids lowering slightly. 'Well, my first for a very long . . . ' Suddenly, her eyes go all watery and she smoothes down her dress in her lap again and gets up from her seat. 'You'll have at least a glass of water, won't you?' she says, wiping an arm across her eyes as she goes to run the tap. 'Hot day like this.'

'I – yes, OK,' I say as she brings two glasses to the table. She sits down and stares into her glass.

'So it's your first year in this apartment?' I prompt her.

Mrs Smith glances up at me as if she's just remembered I'm there. 'It is, yes,' she says briskly. 'That's all there is to it, you see? You got it wrong. Your friend changed her apartment, told you the wrong number. It happens all the time. I'm sure you'll find her. Why don't you ask someone which apartment she has now?'

'I don't need to – I found her!'

Mrs Smith does this really weird thing. Somehow she manages to look relieved and disappointed all at the same time. 'Well, that's wonderful!' she says. 'So you *did* make a mistake!'

She says this as though it's a statement, but the way she's looking into my eyes makes it feel like a question, a challenge – a test. *What's the right answer?*

Something inside my stomach is playing leapfrog. Can I really tell her what's going on? I don't even know this woman. What makes me think she can help? Just because she said she's always felt alone? She could have meant *anything* by that. Why on earth did I think she meant that everything around her suddenly skipped forward a year and left her behind? *How* crazy would it sound if I said that out loud!

'Things have changed,' I say carefully, watching her face for a reaction.

'It happens, you know. Life moves on. Things do change,' Mrs Smith says back, just as carefully. She tightens her lips. 'People get forgotten,' she adds, that sharp edge coming back into her voice.

'No, I don't mean that. I mean she's changed a *lot*. And so have I. I'm not who I was. Or I am, but—'

'You're talking in riddles, child,' Mrs Smith says. 'Spit it out – what are you trying to tell me?'

'She was a year older than I remember!' I burst out before I can stop myself. 'And I am as well! Everything – ' I stop to take a breath. 'It's all moved on. It's all changed. I've lost a year of my life and I don't know where it's gone!'

Mrs Smith looks as though I've slapped her. Her cheeks have gone white, sucked in, her eyes dark and hollow. 'You what?' she says, in a shaky voice.

'I – I don't know what's happened to the whole of last year,' I repeat, less certainly. And then I realise what the look is on her face. She's looking at me as though I'm mad. She thinks I'm a complete and utter crazy loon who shouldn't be allowed to wander around freely.

She stands up and takes a step away from the table. That's it – she's going to call someone, have them take me away. She probably thinks I'm dangerous.

I'm a fool! Just because some lonely woman confessed to me that she's always felt a bit lost, I decide to spill my guts on her kitchen table and make her think I'm a raving lunatic! I have to salvage the situation quickly, before she calls the police and gets someone to cart me away to a safe house with padlocks on the doors.

I try to smile. 'Hey – I'm only joking,' I say. 'Ha ha. Just being silly. I mean, obviously I haven't lost a year of my life! Ha ha, just my little joke.'

Mrs Smith grips the back of her chair. 'You were joking?' she whispers, her words tight like a taut piece of old rope that could snap at any moment. '*Joking?*'

I try to smile again. I know I probably look even more like a demented idiot, but just hearing myself say those words – it was crazy to say them out loud. And to a complete stranger as well! What was I *thinking*?

I need to get out of here. I get up and carefully push my chair under the table.

'Look, I'm really sorry,' I say. 'It was just a joke. A – a dare. Playing around. I'm sorry. It wasn't true. Sorry.'

She nods. Her grip has tightened on the back of her chair. She's furious with me for playing a joke on her, and I'm not surprised.

'I'll go then,' I say, backing away to the door. 'I'm really sorry.' I repeat.

'A dare,' she says, her voice trembling.

'Yep. Sorry. Just kids, you know . . . ?'

'Of course.'

'I'm sorry,' I say one last time. And then, before she has the chance to say another word – or reach for the phone – I grab the door handle, swing it open and get the heck away from there.

My brain is in a scramble as I get to the lifts. I press the button. I can hear electrical whirring sounds behind the door but the lift doesn't appear. I feel really bad about making Mrs Smith think I was playing a joke on her – but what else could I do? It's better than having her think I'm crazy and go and tell my parents I need locking up.

I'm about to head towards the stairs when I hear a clunking noise behind me. The same clunking noise as earlier. It's the old lift.

I yank the door open, pull the gate across and step into the lift. I need to get away from here before Mrs Smith comes after me or tells anyone what just happened. In fact, I need to get away from everyone.

Clanking and heaving, the lift slowly takes me back downstairs.

Once outside, I find myself walking up a lane at the back of Riverside Village. I don't even know where I'm going. I'm just walking along in a blind daze, trying to work out what's happened to my life – where it's gone, if I'll ever get it back.

How can I have lost a whole year?

My thoughts jangle as I walk and walk. After a while I realise I've come to an unfamiliar patch at the start of the woods. I'd better get back. Dad said not to stay out long. I need to get back and look after Craig – and Thea. The thought of my little baby sister almost makes me smile.

I quicken my pace and head back to the apartment.

'Where on earth have you *been*?' Dad yells before I'm even halfway through the door. He slams it behind me after practically pulling me into the apartment. What is his *problem*?

'Blimey, Dad, I'm not late, am I?'

'Not late? Not *late*?' Dad sputters. 'Lydia, get your coat!' he calls to Mum.

'You've got hours yet,' I say. 'What time's the table booked for anyway?'

'Table? What table?'

'Your anniversary dinner.'

Dad stares at me. 'You think we're going out for a meal? Craig, come on!'

'I thought it was just the two of you?'

'The two of us? What are you talking about?'

Mum appears in the hall. She leans back against the doorway. 'Jenni, where've you been?' she asks gently. Her face is starched white, and streaked with damp marks. But that's not the weirdest thing.

The weirdest thing is her stomach. Her huge, round, eight months pregnant stomach. 'Thea,' I say simply, staring at her belly.

Mum pulls a strand of hair out of her eyes. 'What?'

'The – the baby.'

Mum's hands are wrapped round her stomach and she winces and closes her eyes.

'Are you OK?' I ask.

She nods, breathing tightly. 'Just a bit of cramp,' she says. 'Come on, we need to go.'

I look at Mum, then at Dad. 'Go where?' I ask.

'Mum, Dad, what's going on?'

'Craig! Turn that television off NOW!' Dad yells. Turning to me, he snaps, 'We'll tell you in the car.'

'For heaven's sake, Tom. This isn't the kids' fault, you know,' Mum says gently.

'*What's* not our fault? Where are we going?' I ask.

They both ignore me. 'I know it's not the children's fault,' he says. 'I'm sorry, all of you. I just think we should get there. They're our best friends.'

Mum nods, still holding on to her stomach.

'Mum?' I reach out towards her. 'What is it?'

'I'm OK,' she says, breathing quickly. 'Just a bit of – it'll just be the stress. I'm tired. I'm fine, honestly.'

Craig finally slouches out of the living room. Little Craig. The six-year-old Craig of this morning – not the taller Craig I saw last time I was in this room.

I reach up to touch my hair. I clutch at my head. Long. Tied back. But it's *impossible*!

'Are you ready?' Dad says to Craig, totally unaware of the growing panic snarling in my chest.

As he grabs the car keys from the mantelpiece, Dad says, 'Where were you anyway, Jenni? All that fuss you made about going horse riding, and you didn't even turn up.'

Horse riding? My head starts to spin.

'Where were you, Jenni?' Mum and Dad are asking me. I can hear their words, over and over again, blurring, slowing down, speeding up, washing over me. *Where were you, Jenni?*

'I don't know!' I scream eventually, slamming my hands over my ears as Craig slopes past me and out on to the path. 'I don't *know* where I was! OK? I don't know!'

Dad looks at me and shakes his head. 'I don't understand what's going on with you,' he says quietly.

Yeah, you and me both, Dad.

Mum suddenly lets out a sharp gasp, and grips her stomach again. 'Tom, can we get going?' she says. 'I'm not too good here, and this isn't helping.'

Craig runs back into the hallway. 'Can I have a biscuit?' he pipes up before Dad can answer Mum.

Mum smiles as best she can. 'Course you can, darling.'

Dad puts an arm round Mum. 'You OK, love?'

Mum nods. 'Let's just get there.'

'Yes, let's.' He follows Craig into the kitchen. 'Right, come on, you – but just one, OK?'

'Mum. Will you tell me what's happened?' My voice is coming out about ten octaves higher than usual as my throat feels as if it's tightened into a narrow knot. 'Please. Do you two have to go out somewhere before the meal? I'll stay here with Craig if you want. Do you and Dad need to talk? Have you fallen out?' I'm searching my brain for anything I can think of that could explain the mad panic round here. 'You can go for your meal on your own if you like, just the two of you. I don't mind.'

Mum's looking at me as though I just spoke in a foreign language. Maybe I did. Nothing would surprise me today.

Almost nothing.

'There's been an accident,' Mum says carefully. 'Don't get too anxious. I'm sure it'll all be OK, but . . . ' she pauses.

'But what?' The blood is racing through me, pounding in my temples as I clap a hand over my mouth. I know what she's going to say.

'It's Mikey.' She reaches for my free hand, wrapping hers around it. 'He went riding with Autumn. His horse. It threw him off.'

I nod, squeezing my lips tightly shut.

'We don't really know how badly hurt he is, but he – ' Mum breaks off. A strange sound comes out of her throat, as though she's choking. She swallows. 'They thought he was all right. He got worse, very quickly – and then they had to wait. The ambulance was late; no one was there. Jenni, poor little Mikey ended up waiting *two hours*.' This time, the choke turns into a sob.

'Two hours for what?' I hold my breath as the hallway starts to spin away from me.

'To get to hospital.'

I don't respond. My body has turned to stone.

'I should have been there,' Mum whispers. 'I could have helped. I could have done something. I was late. The candle museum – it took longer than I thought, and with the baby . . . ' Her voice trails away.

'He's in the right place now,' I say woodenly.

She shakes her head. 'I'm a first aider. Your dad and I – we did the course together. That's the whole point of it. To be there. And I wasn't. I wasn't,' she croaks.

I force myself to speak. 'You didn't know, Mum. It's hardly your fault,' I say, numb and frozen.

She nods, then pulls a tissue from her pocket. 'We need to go now. Are you ready? Are you OK?'

Am I OK? I nearly laugh. The only thing that stops me is that if I do, I think I'll scream and scream and I won't be able to stop. 'Yeah,' I make myself say eventually. 'Are you?'

She smiles and dabs at her eyes. 'Come on, let's get going.'

Dad and Craig are back. 'Ready?' Dad asks, then he opens the front door and takes Mum's arm.

Two minutes later, we're on the road. Craig gets a couple of matchbox cars out of his little rucksack. Running them up and down his legs, he crashes them into each other, shouting out action film sound effects. Dad grips the wheel with white fists and drives to the hospital at nearly twice the speed limit.

No one asks him to slow down.

8

Dad's at the reception, asking for information about Mikey. I'm waiting in the foyer on some blue plastic seats with Mum, who's pretty much doubled over in her seat.

'Mum, are you OK?' I ask.

'I'm fine, love,' she says. 'I just want to know Mikey's all right.'

I don't think she looks fine at all, but she obviously doesn't want to talk about it.

Craig's racing his cars up and down along the floor. No one stops him.

Dad's back from reception with a piece of paper in his hand. 'Ward 11,' he says. 'We're to follow the orange signs.'

We make our way to Ward 11 – but when we get there, they tell us Mikey's been transferred to the High Dependency Unit. Mum makes that choking noise again when we hear this. 'Tom, I need to sit down,' she says. She looks really pale.

'Mum, I think you could do with seeing a doctor yourself,' I say.

Dad takes her hand. 'Lyd, what's wrong?'

'I'm fine. Please stop fussing, everyone. It's only a bit of indigestion; I'm sure I'll live. My best friend's son has just had a terrible accident. Nothing matters right now except that, all right?'

Dad and I exchange glances and he shrugs. 'As long as you're sure.'

All I can think about is her words. *Just had an accident.* My head is spinning so hard I'm beginning to feel dizzy. I've seen my baby sister, who Mum probably still thinks is a boy. I've seen Autumn and her parents, their lives in tatters because of what's happening in front of my eyes. But when I saw them, this had happened a year ago!

Even if I've now got my memory back, it would still have happened a year ago. So I know my problem isn't that I've got amnesia. Which just leaves me with one question.

If I didn't lose my memory – what on earth happened to me?

The thoughts fizz and crash in my head, eventually grinding into nothingness. I walk through white corridors, my mind blank like the walls.

'This is it. High Dependency Unit,' Dad reads from a sign over two pale blue fire doors.

'Are we allowed in?' I ask.

Mum looks round. 'I'll check with the nurse.' She goes over to the reception desk and talks to a nurse who smiles briskly, tucking her blonde hair under a slide as she nods and points to the fire doors.

Mum comes back towards us. 'She says we can see him for a little bit, but he's not awake.' She pauses as her voice catches. 'His parents have just nipped out to phone and tell their families what's happened. Autumn's inside.'

The nurse is behind her. 'I'll come in with you.'

'You go,' Dad says. 'I'll stay out here with Craig.'

My legs start to give way as we walk towards the doors. Mikey's going to be on the other side. In a hospital bed. Autumn beside him, not knowing what's going to happen to him.

Mum takes my hand. 'You ready to be there for her, Jenni?'

How can I be ready to be there, ready to see what's on the other side of the door, to see the effect it's going to have on Autumn, on her whole family, when one single thought is making my body tremble and almost cave in on itself?

I've already seen it.

Mikey's lying in a bed in the middle of a dark room. He looks tiny, swamped by monitors and machines with dancing lights, jagged lines darting up and down on a computer. Autumn's beside him, leaning over and holding tightly on to his hand. She looks up when we come in and I rush over and wrap my arms around her.

'Oh Autumn, I'm so sorry,' I say.

Just then an alarm bleeps beside the bed and I turn to the nurse, panicked. The nurse pats my arm. 'It's OK. The bleeping is just to give us information. There's nothing wrong.'

Nothing wrong? My best friend's brother is lying on his back in a hospital bed, a drip sticking out of his hand, a brace round his neck, bandages on his head. Nothing wrong?

Tears rush into my eyes, spilling out, flowing down my cheeks. I can taste salt as they run into my mouth. Mum's standing next to me, and I grab hold of her hand.

'We can talk to him,' Autumn says. 'He's asleep at the moment, so he won't reply. But they've said he can probably hear us. They're taking him away for some tests in a bit.'

'Sometimes it can help the patient to hear voices of their friends and family,' the nurse says.

I nod as she backs away from the bed, leaving the three of us huddled round Mikey's bed .

I don't know what to say, and I feel so stupid at the thought of speaking to Mikey while he's lying there like this. I try to remember what I normally talk to him about. Computer games? TV programmes?

'Hey, apparently there's going to be a new *Doctor Who* soon,' I say. I look at Autumn and clear my throat, suddenly scared and empty. I've got no words.

'It's OK,' Autumn says, trying to smile. She squeezes my hand and I feel even worse. She shouldn't be having to look after *me*!

Just then, the doors open again and Mr and Mrs Leonard come in.

'Oh, Abby,' Mum cries, rushing over to throw her arms around Autumn's mum. She's wearing jeans, with a shawl wrapped round her shoulders. It falls loose as they part, but she doesn't adjust it. 'I'm so sorry,' my mum says.

Mrs Leonard just looks at her blankly for a minute. 'Not your fault,' she says eventually, her voice thick and dark. It sounds so lifeless, like one of those electronic voice machines. She stares down at her son, two solitary tears making wet tracks down her pale face.

The nurse comes up to us. 'I'm sorry. We can't have this many people in here at the same time.'

'I'll come out with you for a minute,' Mrs Leonard says as Autumn's dad pulls a chair as close to the bed as possible and sits down, lifting Mikey's hand. 'My baby boy,' he says, his voice choked and raw as the nurse leads the rest of us back outside.

Dad and Craig are sitting across the corridor, reading a comic together. Craig jumps up when he sees us.

'Take him off for a bit, would you?' Mum asks.

Dad picks up Craig's hand. 'Come on, big fella. Let's go find the sweets machine.'

Mrs Leonard looks blankly across at me as we watch Craig and Dad disappear down the corridor. 'Where did you get to?' she asks in the same electronic voice.

'I – I don't know,' I say.

'We waited for you. Waited nearly twenty minutes. Looked for you as well. Thought you'd disappeared into thin air. But you know how Autumn feels about horse riding. So we went. We had two places booked and Mikey was really keen to give it a go, so we let him. Just like his sister. He always loved to try something new . . . ' Her voice dies away. 'Loves,' she corrects herself. 'Not loved. It's not as if he's dead!'

The word lingers in the air. Dead. No, he isn't. And he won't be either. However impossible it is, I know what happens – and even though there isn't much I can give them to help at this time, I can at least offer this.

'He won't die,' I say quietly.

'That's right,' Mum says, clutching her friend's arm. 'You've got to be positive, Abby. There's no point fearing the worst.'

'No, I know,' she replies in a dead voice.

'Has a consultant seen him yet?' Mum asks.

Mrs Leonard nods. 'They're just waiting for the machines to be free and then he's going for some scans.' Her voice breaks as she struggles to carry on. 'They're doing everything they can to speed it up, but they've got a couple of other emergencies.' Her voice cracks on the word. 'He wasn't too bad at first, but now he's asleep – oh, I just can't help worrying.'

'I should have been there, I should have been there,' Mum says, almost to herself.

'Don't blame yourself. He's here now.'

'Oh, Abby.' Mum pulls her close.

'They've told us not to give up,' Mrs Leonard says, tears rolling on to Mum's shoulder. 'They said the next 24 hours are critical.'

'He's not dead,' I say again. 'He's not going to die.'

Mrs Leonard pulls away from Mum. 'Thank you, love. We need to believe.'

I can't bear to see her like this, thinking her son's going to die when I *know* he isn't. I don't know how much comfort it would be if she knew the truth, but at least I know a year from now, he's alive. 'I don't just mean I believe it,' I say. 'I *know* it.'

I think about the last time I saw Mrs Leonard in that dark apartment. 'It's going to be hard,' I say. 'But he's not going to die.'

'Do you really believe that?' she whispers as Mum puts an arm round her shoulder.

'I know it.'

'Thank you.' She squeezes my arm. 'You're right,' she says. 'We've got to have faith.'

I want to tell her it's not just faith; I really do know for sure what's going to happen! But of course I can't tell her that. It's hard enough trying to convince *myself* it's true.

Mum suddenly grabs her stomach again, wincing as though she's been punched right in the stomach. This time she completely doubles over.

'Lydia?' Mrs Leonard's forehead creases up as she looks at Mum. 'Are you all right?'

Mum nods, gasping with pain. 'I'm fine,' she says.

'Lydia.' Mrs Leonard looks seriously at Mum.

'It's nothing,' Mum replies. 'It's hardly important right now. All right?' But then she winces again, and seems to be struggling to breathe.

'That's it. I'm getting a doctor,' Mrs Leonard says. She rushes over to the reception desk and talks to the nurses. A moment later, they're by Mum's side. Mum's doing this really weird fast breathing thing and can hardly speak.

'Mrs Green, we're going to get you to a bed,' one of the nurses says.

The other one turns to me. 'Do you want to get your dad, love?'

I run up the corridor in the direction that Dad and Craig went earlier. Round a bend at the end of the corridor, I spot Dad ambling back toward me with a chocolate-faced Craig.

'Dad! Come quickly – it's Mum!' I say.

Dad grabs Craig's hand and runs towards me.

It all happens really quickly after that. Mum's already on a trolley by the time we get back to them. Dad hands Craig to me and disappears up the corridor holding her hand as she's wheeled off somewhere.

'Stay here,' Dad calls back over his shoulder. 'And don't let Craig out of your sight.'

Just then, there's more beeping from inside Mikey's room. This time, it's louder, and it doesn't stop. His dad runs out at the same time as one of the nurses rushes in. A moment later, she's back on the reception desk, pressing a button on the wall. 'Doctor to HDU. Code Blue. Doctor to HDU.'

And then they've all gone. Mum and Dad have disappeared round one hospital corner and the nurse has joined my best friend and her family, sitting on the other side of a hospital door. Two doctors come running round the corner and up the corridor. They don't even see me as they burst into the High Dependency Unit.

I do the only thing I can do.

I stand in the corridor, hold tightly on to Craig's hand, and let the tears run freely down my face.

As soon as we get back to the apartment, Dad switches the TV on. Mum's still at the hospital. The doctors said she might have gone into early labour and they wanted to keep an eye on her.

'Can I watch the kids' channel?' Craig asks, settling on the floor with his cars.

'After the news,' Dad says.

I make some tea while Dad watches the news and Craig drives his cars all over the furniture. I work in silence. My mind's too full of impossible questions for me to say anything out loud. And Dad certainly won't have any of the answers so there's no point in trying to say anything.

'Jenni!' Dad leaps off the sofa. 'Jenni, come in here!'

He's turning the telly up as I join him in the living room.

'It's the local news,' he says. 'Look.'

There's a close up shot of a young woman with a horse, holding it by its bridle. They're standing by a river. The horse nudges her with its head while she's talking. It's got a dark brown nose with a thin white stripe running all the way down. The woman looks serious.

' . . . all completely devastated,' she's saying. 'Angus has never done anything like this before. None of our horses have.'

The camera switches to a man in a suit. Young and angular, he holds a microphone close to his mouth as he speaks. 'And what happened next?' he asks earnestly.

I edge closer to the television, sitting on the floor, mouth open, right in front of the screen, gawping silently at it. I feel like Craig. Dad's standing silently behind me.

'We were out on a hack,' the woman says. 'We were crossing a river near Mile End Farm when it happened. Angus was galloping so fast towards the edge of the field that he didn't even see the river. Just went ploughing down the bank, throwing the child off in the process.'

'What kind of a state was the boy in?'

'Well, that's the thing. We all thought he was fine. He got up, almost straight away. He'd hurt his head a bit, but other than that, he said he was all right. So he rode back on my horse with me, and the other trek leader took Angus back alongside her horse. We went nice and slowly back to the stables.'

'So when did you realise it was more serious?'

The woman pauses and the camera moves in closer on her face. 'It was when we got back,' she says. 'I helped him off the horse, and he couldn't stand up. He lost his balance – then he was sick.'

'And that was when you called the ambulance?'

The woman nods. 'We would have taken him ourselves but Bob – the other riding instructor – had taken the jeep, and we'd come back early from the hack, so none of the parents had arrived yet.'

Back to the interviewer. 'And I believe there was a bit of an issue with the ambulance?'

The woman's face flushes. 'There was a mix up with the address. There's a Moor*field* Stables on the other side of town. We're Moor*side*.' The woman looks down. 'Some of the parents had started to arrive by that point – but we kept thinking the ambulance would be there any minute so we kept waiting for it. I should have double checked,' she says. 'I should have called them as soon as it happened. I should have done *everything* differently.'

The camera zooms in even closer on the woman's face. There are tears in her eyes. After a pause, it pans across to the interviewer. 'Michael Leonard has been taken to Westchurch Hospital where his symptoms have worsened. His condition has been described as critical.'

My throat closes up.

'Doctors say the next 24 hours will determine what this young boy's future is to hold. This is Pete Travers for North Tonight.'

The room suddenly feels dark. Dad switches the telly off, but we both carry on staring at it, as though perhaps it'll come back on and tell us there's been a mistake.

The only noise is Craig whizzing his cars along the radiator and flinging them over the edge to crash on to the floor.

I've been lying in bed for hours but I can't sleep. I can't stop my mind from whirring and spinning. It's like a fairground ride going round and round too fast to jump off. The thoughts all crowd together: Autumn in the future, lifeless and tired, her Mum like a zombie, Mikey in hospital – all of it awful, and all happening the wrong way round.

Everyone older, then younger again. What happened? *How* did it happen?

Stop!

I try a relaxation exercise that Mum once showed me. Focus on my breathing, on the breath coming into my body cold, leaving it warm. Close my eyes, let my tummy swell . . . in . . . out. In . . . out.

It's helping. She has loads of these exercises. She's been using them with the pregnancy. She reckons it helps the baby stay calm.

That's another thing! She's already had the baby. Or she *had* – or she will. Which is it? I'm jerked awake again, with the thoughts tumbling on top of each other. It's no use. I'm not going to get to sleep.

I switch on my bedside lamp and glance across at Craig. He's sprawled out on his back, arms above his head, breathing in deep grunts, teddies spread out on the pillow, with his favourite, Monkey, lying next to his cheek.

I slide open my bedside drawer and pull out my diary.

I've had the most horrific day of my life, I write. *In fact, I've had the two most horrific days of my life – both on the same day!*

I write down everything that happened, every single event of the day: going to Autumn's apartment and that woman being there, the old lift, the man telling me to go downstairs, seeing Autumn and her Mum in that dark room, rushing to hospital – everything. I pour it all out, pages and pages of it.

It's only when I stop writing and read it back that I realise something. As a shiver judders and slithers through my body, it comes to me. The moment it all changed.

I know how it happened.

9

The moment a hint of daylight breaks into the room, I'm out of bed. I've spent the whole night lying awake staring at the ceiling, waiting for morning. At least, it feels as though I have. I must have fallen asleep at some point as I woke up sweating from a bad dream. I was running after Autumn, but she kept running away from me. She ran round a corner and disappeared. When I caught up with her, she'd turned into Mikey. He was laughing as he ran, and looking back at me over his shoulder. He didn't know that he was heading towards the edge of a cliff. I kept trying to warn him but he couldn't hear me. Mum was at the edge of the cliff, holding a baby in the air. Any second, Mikey was going to run into them and all three would go over the cliff – and then I woke up.

I shake the dream out of my head as I get up. I'd wanted to go out as soon as I'd realised what had happened, but I couldn't. On top of everything, I simply didn't have the nerve to go out chasing answers in the middle of a pitch black night.

Craig's snoring softly. He shuffles and turns over, kicking his quilt to the floor. I lift it and gently place it back over him. Then I get my baggiest jeans and the biggest t-shirt I've got out of the cupboard and slip them on. The alarm clock's red lights catch my eye: 6.51.

There's a note on the living room table.

Hospital rang in night. Mum's gone into labour! Look after Craig. Will be back as soon as poss. Dad xxx

She's a month early. Is it OK to go into labour so soon? I silently pray that she'll be OK – and then I realise I know she will be. I've seen the baby!

Look after Craig. Does that mean I have to stay here?

No. I have to do this. I have to know for sure. And I won't be long. I scrawl a note for Craig, and put it next to Dad's.

Craig, just nipped out to get a few things. Get yourself some breakfast and watch telly and I'll see you soon, love Jenni xx

I slink out of the house like a burglar, silently closing the front door behind me, and head for Autumn's block.

The entrance hall is empty. It looks the same as

it's looked every day, the same as it looks every year. The marble walls, the fountain trickling out behind a glass panel, the archway to the ground floor corridor. The lift. The one we've always used. And next to it, the other one: the one that's never worked. Never until yesterday.

I walk towards it and catch my breath. My heart's thumping hard in my chest as I step carefully inside and slide the doors closed behind me, slicing away the light. I can't see the buttons properly. I fumble along the walls, the numbers slowly growing clearer as my eyes get used to the dim light. My body is alive with prickles zinging up and down, lighting up every nerve ending in my back, my neck, my arms.

I know it's impossible. I know it can't be true. But I also know it *is* true. It happened; there's no other explanation.

The lift didn't only take me up a floor – it took me up a year as well.

What if Autumn had lived on the second floor and I'd gone up two floors to see her? Would it have taken me forward two years instead of one?

Perhaps another year on from that awful time, things will get back to normal. Perhaps we'll all be happy again.

I need to know.

The buttons are clearly visible now my eyes have got used to the gloom. As I stare at them, I know there's only one way to answer the questions shooting around my mind.

With a shaking arm, I reach out, and press the button marked '2'.

The lift stops. I drag the doors open, run to the corridor and check the apartment numbers. 210, 211, 212 . . .

I run down the stairs. At the first floor, I pause and look down towards Autumn's old apartment. Before I've even thought about it, I'm marching along the corridor. I'm not going to wimp out of it this time. I need to ask some straight questions – and I need some honest answers.

I stop outside apartment 110. My chest feels as though there's someone inside it, banging their fists on my ribs. I knock three times on the door, and a second later it flies open.

'It's you! I *knew* you'd come back!' Mrs Smith smiles broadly and grabs me. She pulls me towards her, squashing me in a tight, bony hug.

I pull away. 'What's that about?' I ask, stepping back to look at her. Is she older? It's hard to tell. She's wearing different clothes but –

That's when I realise. My clothes. I look down at my exposed ankles, my jeans stopping a good five centimetres short of my shoes, my wrists bare where my t-shirt stops.

'Come on in, Jenni.' Mrs Smith holds the door open for me.

'Can I use your bathroom?' I ask. I need to be sure. She motions me into the apartment.

In the bathroom, I stare at myself. It's *so* weird. It's as if I'm looking at myself, but looking at someone else at the same time. It's hard to even put my finger on what's different. My face looks about the same. A bit thinner, perhaps. My hair's still quite short, but it's got tinges of colour in it. Highlights? Mum's let me dye my hair? Well, that's one good thing anyway. It suits me.

This is me at 14. This is what I'll look like. I can't stop staring.

'You all right in there, Jenni?'

I've not got time to sit around examining my looks! I need to sort this out. 'Just coming,' I call.

She's waiting for me at the kitchen table, a couple of glasses of orange juice in front of her. She points to one of them. 'I got you some juice,' she says with a nervous laugh. 'Not just water like last time.'

I sit down. 'Thanks,' I say, taking a sip.

She watches me drink. 'About last time,' she says. 'I'm sorry I was so awful with you.'

'You weren't awful,' I say quickly.

She shakes her head. 'No, I was. Jenni. Please let me apologise.' She smiles, and her eyes are so full of sadness and regret that I instantly want to give her whatever she needs.

'OK,' I say. 'Thank you.'

'I thought you were playing a joke on me, you see.

But then the more I thought about it, the more convinced I became that I was wrong – and then it was too late to do anything about it. I prayed you would come back,' she says. 'I couldn't come to you. Couldn't say what I wanted to say in front of your family and friends. I wanted to tell you everything.'

'Tell me what?'

'After you came here . . . '

'Last year?' I ask. I realise I'm holding my breath while I wait for her to answer.

'Yes,' she says. 'last year.'

My heart thuds to a stop. I thought she knew the truth. I must have misunderstood her. 'But—'

'Or in your case . . . ' Mrs Smith leans forwards and peers into my face, 'yesterday.'

'Really? You know?' I swallow hard.

'Yes – I know it all,' she says in a whisper. 'I probably knew the first time you came round. I wasn't going to admit it, though. Not to you at any rate, not even to myself. I mean, it's not possible, is it?'

'No,' I say numbly. *She understands! She believes me!*

Mrs Smith holds my eyes. For a long time, neither of us says anything. Then she takes a quick breath and speaks quickly. 'You lost a year, didn't you? The rest of the world carried on, leaving you behind – and you don't know where it went, or how to get back. And it happened right here.' She leans forward, sliding my glass out of the way to take hold of my hands. 'It's true, isn't it?' she says, her eyes as tight as her voice. 'I'm not just a rambling old fool. Tell me I'm not. Tell me I've not lost my mind, Jenni. Tell me it really happened.'

'I . . . How did you know I was telling the truth? What made you so certain I wasn't playing a trick on you?'

Her grip tightens on my hand. 'It is true, then?'

I nod. 'Yes, it's true,' I say.

She gets up from her chair, crossing to the kitchen sink. Looking out of the window, she carries on almost to herself, as though she's forgotten I'm there. 'How could I explain it? How do you explain something that makes no sense at all?'

'You – you – how . . . ?' I can't finish the question. I don't even know what I'm trying to ask.

'How did I know it had really happened to you as you said?' She smiles sadly. 'I saw it in your eyes. The shock, the disbelief, the questions. I've only ever seen that expression once in my life.' She looks up at me. 'And you know when that was, don't you?'

I suddenly realise what she's saying. At least I think I do. But she *can't* be!

'It was when I saw my own reflection,' she says. 'How do you explain something like that? I was just a child, like you. I had no idea what was going on, no one to explain. I couldn't tell anyone.' She slides back into her chair, facing me. 'Do you understand, Jenni? No one. No way of knowing what had happened, how, why . . . nothing. A year of my life gone. And all I knew was this: it happened here.'

'You came here as a child? But I didn't think it existed then.'

'It didn't. Not like this, anyway. It was a hotel. Did you know that?'

I shake my head.

'Just this building. The rest has been built around it over the years. Dilapidated little place it was, back then. My parents brought us here every year.'

'So what happened?' I ask.

'Thirteen years old, I was. Nearly fourteen. Always wanting to be older, wishing my life away. If only I'd known. I remember the night before it happened. I'd been reading a book about a girl who travelled back in time, and I thought wouldn't it be marvellous to be able to travel through time.'

That was what I'd done too! When it happened, I'd just been wishing I could see into the future!

'We always celebrated my birthday here at the hotel,' Mrs Smith carries on. 'I'd been out with my friends in the afternoon, and I came back home to our room. As soon as I walked in the door, I knew something was wrong. The celebrations were taking place – but they were the wrong ones.'

'The wrong ones?'

'The cards. The first one was from my grandparents. I thought they'd made a mistake. *Happy Birthday, darling granddaughter. Fifteen today.* I showed it to my mother, laughing. Said to her, look what they've gone and done. She gave me a strange look. Open the rest of your cards, she said. So I did. I tore the next one open. It was from my Auntie Gladys and Uncle Frank.'

'And it was the same?'

She nods. 'Fifteen today. All of them. It wasn't funny after a while. Wasn't funny at all.'

'And then you saw yourself?'

'I'll never forget it, as long as I live. Mother had given me a hairbrush set. Beautiful it was. Gold trimmings, and padded on the back with a picture of an old English sheepdog.' She pauses. 'There was a hand mirror. That was when I knew for sure. One look. Dropped the mirror right out of my hands I did. It smashed to pieces right there on the table. Mother wasn't half cross.'

'Seven years bad luck,' I murmur.

'Oh, I had much more than that, Jenni. That was just the start of it. Anyway, I went to the bathroom, tried to calm myself down.'

'Just like me,' I say. 'And it made it worse?'

'Absolutely. Seeing my reflection like that. It was like the hall of mirrors. Looking at yourself, but it's not really yourself, not the person you know. It's a freaky distortion, a shadow stretched by late afternoon sun. Or a hallucination, a nightmare. You try to peer at it sideways, try to catch it out. But it won't be caught.'

'So then what happened?'

'When I came back out, my parents had put the cards up on the mantelpiece. They thought it would cheer me up. Well, they had no idea what was going on, did they? All they could see was that I was unhappy. So they tried to make it better. You know what I did?'

I shake my head.

'Tore them all down. Wiped them off the ledge, then I ripped them into shreds. Every last one. Screaming

128

all the while. Nearly smashed the whole place up. I thought I was losing my mind. So did my parents. They were ever so worried, for a while at any rate.'

'Why only for a while?'

Mrs Smith reaches down to brush invisible crumbs from her dress. 'I gave in, eventually. Played along.'

'What d'you mean, "played along"? What did you do?'

She lets out a heavy sigh. 'After a couple of weeks, I told them I'd made it up. Said I'd put the whole thing on, that it was all about trying to get attention. What else could I do? I couldn't keep putting them through that anguish, so I made up some tripe that they were happy to believe – *desperate* to believe. I lied, basically. And then I carried on lying. Said I remembered everything. Told them everything was normal, apologised, got on with it.'

'With your new life, a year ahead of the one you knew?'

'Exactly. Oh, the punishment I endured for being a liar. If I close my eyes, I can still feel those slaps on the backs of my legs. But it got easier, you know. It does. The gaps are easy to fill in. You just have to learn how to do it. Ask the right questions, in the right way, and people will tell you everything you need to know.' She turns away, but not before I've noticed that the edge of her eye is damp. 'Or nearly everything.'

'What d'you mean?'

'I mean, you can lie to others, you can even lie to yourself. You can very nearly convince yourself things aren't really how you see them, didn't really happen, haven't sent you to the very edge of your sanity. But I'll tell you something Jenni.'

'What?' I hold my breath.

'You can't lie to your spirit.' She clenches her teeth, raising her head in a defiant nod. 'When you try to do that, you die inside, Jenni.'

'Is that what you did?'

She tightens her jaw. 'I didn't just lose a year. I lost everything.' She half smiles as she looks out of the window. 'I was in love with him. I was going to tell him that night.'

'In love with who?'

'I said to myself, once I'm fourteen, I'll tell him. Every year, I saw him. I knew he was the one. Right from the start. But I thought, you can't be in love at ten years old, or eleven or twelve or even thirteen. That's what they all said, anyway. My parents laughed at me. My friends thought I was loopy. Boys! They weren't interested in *boys*! Well, nor was I, really. Not boys. Just the one boy. I told myself, as soon as I'm fourteen, I'm going to tell him.'

'Why fourteen?'

She shakes her head. 'I've asked myself that a thousand times. I don't know. It just sounded older. Old enough. And I thought, if he feels the same way, we'll get married, and then we'll be together forever. Every day, every week, not just one week out of fifty-two.'

'So what happened?'

'I'd seen him the night before. He tried to kiss me.

Well, he'd kissed me before, on my cheek. Lots of times. But it was different this time, I knew it was. He leaned right forward towards me, closed his eyes . . . '

'And?'

'And I ducked. Jerked away from him. You should have seen his face. Looked as though I'd slapped him. I said, no, don't kiss me yet. Not till tomorrow. What happens tomorrow, he asked. I said, it's my birthday, I'll be grown up tomorrow. You can kiss me then.'

'What did he say?'

'He said I was making excuses. Said I didn't really want him to kiss me, and if that was how I felt then he wouldn't bother. I told him, no, you've got it all wrong, but he stormed off.' She tears her gaze away from the window and turns to me. 'I wanted it to be special, you see. I had it all planned. I had to be fourteen. I'd convinced myself of that, for some stupid, stupid reason. I was going to tell him I was in love with him. It was going to be perfect.'

'And?'

'He never tried again.'

'To kiss you?'

'Next time I saw him, I'd lost a year. He hardly spoke to me. Kept walking past me holding hands with another girl. He stopped to kiss *her* once, right in front of me. I saw his eyes, though. Open, they were, right there as he kissed her. *See*, he was saying. *I can get kisses if I want them.*'

'But didn't you tell him?'

Mrs Smith laughs drily. 'Tell him? Tell him what?

That I was sorry but I'd accidentally lost a year of my life and could we take up where we left off? Think he'd have taken me seriously? Anyway, I did try actually. Just once.'

'What did you say?'

'I told him I hadn't meant to push him away that time. Said I wasn't rejecting him. Told him I couldn't really remember what had happened afterwards, and I tried to get him to tell me – to help me fill in the blanks.'

'What did he say?'

'He told me I'd said the same thing before, and he wasn't going to suddenly give me a different reply now. I could only assume he meant that in the year I had no recollection of, I'd tried to explain what had happened that night. But it was obvious he wasn't having any of it. He told me to leave him to get on with his life. I said I didn't want to leave him to get on with anything.'

'And what did he say to that?'

'He started getting angry then. Asked if I thought he was going to hang around while I made a fool of him again, and told me I didn't need to feel sorry for him. Said he had a new girlfriend now, so I didn't need to worry about him bothering me any more.'

'So he never knew what really happened?'

Mrs Smith shakes her head. 'I remember the conversation where I tried to explain it to him, as if it were yesterday. We were standing in the foyer downstairs, in front of the lift.'

'The lift!' I gasp. *Does she know that was how it happened?*

'As we stood there, I suddenly realised – that was it,' she continues before I get the chance to say anything. 'The moment things had changed. It was the lift! I grabbed his hand and dragged him inside with me. Told him what I suspected. Told him all of it. I was so happy! All we had to do was go back a year – together. Everything was going to be OK. More than OK – it was going to be wonderful! I was going to get my life back. And he would get to live that year all over again – but as my boyfriend this time!'

'So what happened?' I ask, entranced.

Mrs Smith pauses for a long time. 'He looked into my eyes so hard and so deep that I mistook his look. I thought it was excitement, passion – a realisation that we could have everything we wanted, everything we had talked about.'

'And what was it?'

'I don't know. Fury, hurt,' she says flatly. 'Do you know what he did, Jenni?'

I shake my head, anxious for her to go on.

'He got out the pen knife he always carried around with him in his pocket and went over to the control box in the corner of the lift. Working at the edge of it with his knife, he levered it open. And then, before I even knew what was happening, he switched to the sharpest blade, reached into the box and pulled out the wires inside it. Then he said, this is what I think of your nonsense, and cut every wire in the box. No one makes a fool of me and then comes back to gloat about it, he said.'

'But that's horrible of him!' I butt in.

Mrs Smith shakes her head. 'It sounds it. But it wasn't like him at all. He was always so gentle and kind. He was hurt, Jenni. He needed to hit back at me and didn't know any other way to do it. Don't think badly of him.'

'OK. I understand,' I say quietly. 'So then what happened?'

'I said I'm *not* gloating Bobby, I *promise* I'm not. But he never believed me. All he knew was that I'd rejected him and that was that. He'd had a whole year to think about it. A year that I had no recollection of – a year of my life that took place without me!'

'Everyone around you acting as though you've spent the last year with them – but you don't know anything about it. It's awful isn't it?'

'Worse than awful,' Mrs Smith agrees.

'But I still don't understand how it works,' I say. 'I mean, if the missing year existed for everyone around us, but not for you or me, then was that year real? Did it happen or not? And what about the past that you've left behind? Do you disappear from that completely, or carry on existing in two places at the same time?'

'Jenni, I've spent over thirty years asking myself questions like these. I know that you can't disappear from the past completely, or else by the time I turned up on my fifteenth birthday, they'd have had search parties out looking for me for the last twelve months! And I know they never did that.'

'But if I didn't disappear, why didn't I turn up at Autumn's house?'

Mrs Smith shakes her head. 'There could be a hundred different answers to that question. Perhaps you *do* disappear, just for a short while, as you travel from one time to another. Or perhaps we both just slipped into the timeline that was always there, and was always going to be there, and no one disappeared from anywhere. Perhaps the past kind of starts again once you land in the future.'

'The past with all the bits we'll never know about because we simply weren't there to experience them,' I add.

'Exactly. The truth could even be that Jenni from a year ago was called away by someone before she got to Autumn's apartment,' Mrs Smith goes on. 'Maybe she got distracted for ten minutes, and by the time she went round to Autumn's it was too late and they'd gone without her. The fact of the matter is . . . ' She pauses for a moment.

'That I'm never going to know,' I finish for her.

'I don't think you ever will,' she agrees. 'Just as I'll never know exactly what happened in my missing year either. But I'll tell you something else I've discovered. It doesn't matter! There are *always* going to be some questions you can answer, and some that you can't and which will send you crazy if you keep trying. Not all questions *have* an answer, Jenni – and even with the ones that do, not all of their answers make sense to our simple human minds.'

She's right. Understanding the ins and outs of exactly why and how this has happened isn't important. What matters is the fact that it *has*. It happened to Mrs Smith; it's happened to me. And however complicated and impossible all of this is, there's one simple truth at the heart of it. Both of us ended up in a future we wished we could change.

My head is swimming. I want to ask her so many things. I want her story to have a happier ending.

'Did you ever see him again?' I ask.

'Never. It was too late. He didn't want me. All I knew was that as far as he was concerned, I'd rejected him and then tried to make a fool out of him with some ridiculous story. I don't blame him for not believing me. But I wished and wished he would.'

'What happened next?'

'I got into such a state, my parents cut the holiday short. It put them off the place for good.'

'So you never came back?'

'Never. At least, not till last year, when you saw me.'

'Last year? You mean yesterday?' I say without thinking.

'Takes a bit of getting used to, doesn't it?' she says quietly.

'So why did you come back at all?'

She doesn't answer.

'Was it to look for him?' I ask.

'You'll think I'm an old fool. As crazy as my poor old parents thought I was, back then.'

'I won't. I promise.'

'Do you know something, Jenni? You are the first person I've told any of this to, in my entire life. Do you realise that?'

I try to imagine keeping something like that a secret for my whole life. It would be like always wearing a mask over your face, which everyone believed was the real you. You would be the only person who knew it wasn't – and who knew that you could *never* take it off.

'I'm sorry,' I say eventually. I don't know what else to say.

'We had this thing,' she says, staring out of the window again. 'Used to joke about it. We'll come here when we're fifty, he'd say. We'll buy this place and run it together. We'll be married then, I'd reply, and he'd throw grass on me. I never forgot, though. All my life. I mean – yes, of course I moved on. He wasn't my only love. But he was the first – and the deepest – and my heart never gave up the corner it had reserved for him all those years ago. So I did.'

'You did what?'

'I came back when I was fifty! There, now. Stupid old fool, like I said. As if he'd be here. As if he'd remember.' She shakes her head and laughs. 'Can you imagine that? Bought a timeshare apartment and everything. Couldn't get rid of the darned thing till now.'

'Get rid of it?'

'What use is a place like this to someone like me? No, I've sold it on now. Made a loss, of course, but it's nothing to the losses I've had. I'll be off after this week. Won't come here again. Nothing here for me now, is there? Not that there ever was. I know that now.' She looks away and seems to be looking far away in the distance. 'D'you know what I did last night?' she asks with a wry smile.

'What did you do?'

'Wrote him a letter. Silly mumbo jumbo my daughter tells me to do when people upset me. She says write it in a letter, then address it to them, but don't send it. She reckons it gets rid of the feelings.'

She points to a writing pad at the other end of the table. 'So I wrote a letter. My daughter says I have to destroy it. I will do, later. I'll go down to the weir and throw the silly thing in. Get him out of my head once and for all and that'll be that. Over and out.'

'You never forgot him,' I say quietly.

She shakes her head. 'Bobby was the one, Jenni. Was for me, at any rate, even if the feeling wasn't mutual. The one that shone through the others. Sounds like something out of a bad film, doesn't it?'

'Did you never meet anyone else?'

'Oh, yes. I got married, went my way. Divorced, too. Because it *wasn't* a film. It was real life, and the girl doesn't always get her boy in the real world. I moved on, lived my life. But there's always been a sense of – I don't know, unfinished business I suppose you'd call it. Knowing that everything could have turned out so differently – and wishing more than anything that I could have my time again and turn it into the life I really wanted.'

'The one where you married Bobby?'

She smiles. 'I used to write it all over my homework books: Irene Barraclough. I thought it sounded quite good.'

'Barraclough?'

'Bobby Barraclough. That was his name.'

My insides turn cold. 'But there's a Mr Barraclough who works here. He did, anyway, two days ago – or rather, two years ago.'

'Mr Barraclough.' Her face has turned white. 'Bobby Barraclough?'

'I don't know. I've never known his first name. I think he's left now. He said it was going to be his last year. Said he was staying for his fiftieth birthday and then that was it. He'd be off.' As I say the words, the cold feeling seeps and snaps its way through my body. *His fiftieth birthday* – was that why he was leaving? Did it have anything to do with Mrs Smith?

Mrs Smith is staring at me, the colour drained from her cheeks. 'Oh my goodness,' she says. 'Oh my goodness.'

'What? What is it?'

'His fiftieth. *His* fiftieth. I've been such a fool, even more of a fool than I'd thought. I had my whole life to prepare and I got it wrong.'

'Got what wrong?'

'He was a year older than me! I came a year too late!' She gets up and paces the floor. 'It was his last year, you say?'

'I think so.'

'And what was he going to do after that?'

'I – I can't remember. I think he said he was going travelling.'

'With his family? Was he married?'

I try to remember what I know about him. I've only ever seen him on his own. But then you don't take your wife to work with you, do you? 'I don't think so. I don't know,' I say eventually. 'I'm sorry.'

She stops pacing. 'No. *I'm* sorry.' She tries to smile. 'Look at me. Just can't let go, can I? It's over. The silly dream of a silly girl. A silly old woman. There's no going back. It's done now. He's gone. He's moved on and it's time I did the same.'

'But maybe he *hasn't* moved on!' I burst out. 'Maybe that's why he was leaving. Maybe that's why he stayed till then – for you!'

She looks at me, a glint of hope in her eyes. Then she shakes her head. 'No – I'm not going to get silly hopes up over nothing. He's gone now anyway, even if it *was* as you said – which I very much doubt.'

'Come back with me and find out!' I burst out. 'The lift – it's working again!'

'The lift? So I was right – that's how it happened to you, too?'

I nod. And then I remember something else. 'It was the day after he was there.'

'Who was there?'

'Mr Barraclough – he was trying to fix the lift! Maybe that was why! Maybe he was fixing it for you!' I try to remember what he said to me at the time, but I can't. All I can remember is that he didn't make any sense. But maybe he did! Maybe this was exactly what he was talking about.

Mrs Smith runs a hand through her hair and chews her cheek. Then she shakes her head. 'No. I can't do it,' she says.

'Why not?'

'Jenni, your theory is full of "ifs". Far too many to hope that all of them would go my way. There's no going back. I've lived all these years with that as a permanent refrain in the background of my life. You cannot go back. You have to go forward.'

'But what if you—'

She stops me with her hand. 'No, I can't do it. Maybe last year, I would have. Even a couple of days ago, perhaps I might have said yes. I might have dared face another humiliating rejection. But not now. Now I realise why I came here again.'

'Why's that?'

'To let go. To move on. I've made my peace with all of this, and I'm not going to risk shattering that now. I can't, Jenni. Not at my age.'

'But maybe he—'

'No, I can't do it. I won't. My whole life has been about moving forward. I can't go back. And anyway, I don't believe he'll have given me a moment's thought in the last thirty years. Now I'm here, I can see that even more clearly. He's gone. It's too late. He'll have been getting his last jobs done before he left this place behind for good – and that is exactly what I'm going to do.'

'So what happens now?'

'What happens now is that I pack up, I go home, and I get on with my life. It's about time.'

'Will you be OK?'

She picks up the glasses and takes them to the sink. Running the tap, she talks to the window. 'I'll be fine,' she says. 'I've been all right up to now, haven't I? I'll survive.'

As she's talking, my eyes fall on the writing pad. What did she say to him? What's it like to be fifty and in love? I didn't know it was possible!

'Can I see it?' I ask, nervously. *Did I really ask that? Jenni Green doesn't ask things like that!* But then I realise – perhaps Jenni Green isn't the same person she used to be. And I don't just mean a haircut and tighter clothes. I mean something more than that – something inside.

Mrs Smith turns round. 'See what?'

'The letter,' I say, nervously. And then I have a thought. Or half a thought. I don't even know exactly what the thought is, never mind whether or not I could pull it off. I just know that I have to try to do *something*. I can't shake the feeling that Mr Barraclough still loves her like she loves him. I can't persuade her to take the risk and try to find out. But perhaps there's a way *I* can find out. And if I knew what the letter said, maybe somehow that could help. 'Can I read it?' I add. 'To help me understand what you've been through?'

She dries her hands on a towel and comes back to the table. 'Do you know what?' she says, smiling genuinely for the first time since we've been talking. 'I've got an even better idea.'

Then she picks up the pad, tears off the first three sheets and hands them to me. 'Have it,' she says.

I look at the pages of flowery writing in my hand. 'Why?'

'I promised myself I'd write the letter and then dispose of it. I didn't specify how. This way, I get rid of the letter – and you have a permanent reminder.'

'Of what?' I ask.

'Of what happens if you just accept what happens to you, and don't try hard enough to change it. It's too late for me – and maybe it always was. But I don't want you to have a life like mine. Try harder than I did – while you still can!'

I carefully fold her letter in half and put it in my pocket. 'Thank you.'

Mrs Smith smiles and wipes her hands on her dress. 'There we are now,' she says. 'It's done. So, really, I should be thanking *you*.'

'I should get back,' I say as I stand up. Talking to Mrs Smith has given me *some* answers, but I need more. I still need to know how things are going to work out for Autumn's family – and for mine.

She holds out her hands to me as I get to my feet. 'Good luck, Jenni. I hope your life turns out differently from mine.'

'Thank you,' I say as she pulls me towards her and hugs me tight.

'Don't just accept the life you're given,' she says at

143

the door. 'Question everything. Always attempt the impossible. Be brave. Will you do that, for me, Jenni?'

'I will,' I say. 'I wish I could do more than that for you.'

She reaches out and briefly takes my hand. 'I'm OK, Jenni. I'll be fine.'

I nod, I try to smile, and then I turn and head for the stairs.

10

'There you are!'

I'm just coming out the front of Autumn's block as Mum runs over to me. I've taken the stairs as I need to stay here, two years ahead. I have to know what's going to happen.

'Come on,' Mum says.

'Come on what?'

'We're off. I've been looking for you.'

'Off where?'

Mum sighs. 'The ice-cream farm. Come on, Jenni. Craig's in the apartment with Thea. I said I'd only be two minutes. Let's get going.' She smiles. 'I can't wait to see Thea's face when she sees all those ice creams!'

We're outside the ground floor apartment that was Autumn's last year. Is she still there? What's changed? I'm desperate to find out. And I'm desperate to read Mrs Smith's letter too. It feels as if it's burning a hole in my pocket, but I can't read it with Mum and Craig around.

'Do I have to go?' I ask.

Mum's face falls completely flat. 'I thought you liked doing these things. And I thought you liked being with me.'

'I do. Of course I do. It's just I really need to see Autumn.'

Mum sighs again. 'Oh, Jenni. Can't you leave Autumn to her own devices for one morning? I know it's awful of me to say but . . . '

'But what?'

'Well, I know how much she needs you – how much they all do – but just this once, can't you let them get on with things and spend a bit of time with us? Especially with Autumn being so unpredictable at the moment. You've said yourself how hard it's been lately.'

'I have?'

'Well, not in so many words. But I can see that's how you feel. You never come home from her house smiling like you used to.' Mum's face colours instantly. 'I mean – not that I'd expect you to. I'm sorry. I just sometimes wish we could have a bit of the old Jenni back, though.'

You and me both, Mum!

'She's my best friend,' I say.

'I know. Just – well, sometimes it seems a bit like you're acting out of some kind of . . . ' Her voice trails away.

'Some kind of what?'

'Oh, I don't know. It's not for me to say. I've been

bad enough myself. I'm only just starting to get my own act together, you know, now that your dad and I – ' She breaks off and walks away, heading back towards our block. 'Come on, let's get going,' she says.

I catch her up. 'No, tell me,' I say.

Mum stops and turns to me. 'OK, I'll say it. Guilt. Like you can never do enough for her, always trying to make amends, make her life better. I mean, I under-stand – of *course* I do – but sometimes I can't help wondering if it's holding you back from moving on with your own life. It's as though you won't let your-self be happy again until Autumn is.' Mum reaches for my hand. 'And I don't know if that's going to happen for a long time,' she adds softly.

I don't know what to say. All I can think is – so noth-ing's changed.

'Come on, let's go out,' Mum says, still holding my hand as we head back to the apartment. I walk along numbly beside her. I'll have to leave Autumn and my letter till later. It seems Mum needs me as much as Autumn does this time.

'Is Dad coming?' I ask as we approach our apartment.

Mum stops in her tracks. 'Jenni, that's not even funny,' she says, staring at me.

I stare back at her. 'What?'

'Of course your Dad's not coming.'

'Why not?' I ask. In the silence before she replies, I realise I'm holding my breath.

'Oh, Jenni. Please don't start this again.'

'Start *what* again?'

'We've been through it so many times. This is *my* week with you and Craig.'

My stomach turns cold. 'Your week? You . . . you've split up?' I say numbly.

Mum stops on the doorstep, looking into my eyes. 'I thought you were all right with this,' she says, more gently. 'We agreed it was for the best. It's better for you and Craig in the long run, don't you think?'

'What's best?'

'It's not good for you to be in such a tense atmosphere.'

'Tense atmosphere? There's *never* a tense atmosphere at home – you and Dad get on great!'

'Jenni, that's kind of you to say – as I know a lot of it was my fault. But you don't need to pretend. We all know what it's been like.'

'What what's been like?' I ask. *What's happened to my family?*

Mum just shakes her head. 'Jenni, where have you been for the past two years?'

'I . . . ' *Yeah. Good question, Mum.*

'We've both tried our best, but since, well, you know, since Mikey – '

A sword slices into my chest and I catch my breath.

'It just hasn't been the same,' Mum goes on, oblivious. *Since Mikey what? Is he still alive? What's happened to him?* I can't ask outright. Mum will seriously worry about me then. She's still talking.

'We've both changed, and it's good that we've acknowledged that. Things just aren't right between us any more. We all know it. This is for the best, Jenni.'

She takes my hand. 'And I've been coping with things better, with Thea and everything, now we've not got all the drama. You've said so yourself.' She tries to smile. 'And we're happier,' she says. I don't know if she's convincing herself, but looking at her eyes, she's certainly not convincing me. 'At least, we will be,' she adds, maybe reading my mind. 'It'll take time. But you'll get used to it. We all will.'

She turns back to the apartment. 'Come on. Let's just get going. It'll be OK,' she adds with half a smile.

Craig shuffles into the car beside me. He looks so different! He's wearing jeans and a lime green t-shirt. His hair has been chopped into a little crew cut. Trendy little eight-year-old. I can't help smiling. He sticks his tongue out at me as he pulls the door closed.

Thea sits in the child seat that I remember using for Craig when he was her age. She shakes her legs and points out of the window, shouting 'Baa, baa!' every time we pass a sheep, and 'Eee orr' when we pass a field of horses. Her innocent delight briefly takes my mind off everything else, and for a few moments in the car, I relax and smile, allowing myself to get lost in her world.

But then we get to the ice-cream farm, and while we walk around, I can't concentrate on anything. I just want to get back and see Autumn. I can't bear not knowing what's going on for her.

Mum, Craig and Thea sample virtually every flavour between them. Craig has at least three helpings of the raspberry pavlova and Mum goes back for seconds of the lavender, the honeycomb and the chocolate orange and Cointreau. Thea covers every bit of her face and clothing in brightly coloured goo, much to everyone's delight.

I get a vanilla ice cream, just so Mum doesn't hassle me and worry if I'm OK. But I can't eat it. My insides are too churned up and my throat feels too thick, so I just take the occasional lick, and knock bits of it into the bin when no one's looking.

I can't stop worrying about what's going to happen when we get back. I can't stop thinking about Autumn, and wanting to know what's happened to her and her family. Wishing and hoping and praying that, despite what Mum was saying earlier, things have changed for them. That Mikey's got better, that Autumn's OK, that her parents have got their lives back on track. Maybe Mum was exaggerating before. Maybe she was wrong. I have to find out. Not only has all that happened, but now it turns out my parents have split up too! This future world is getting worse and worse. The only good thing about it is Thea. There has to be something else good in this reality. There *has* to be.

But my mind keeps hurling horrible thoughts and questions around. What if I *can't* get back? I keep thinking about how Mrs Smith got stuck in the future. What if that happens to me too?

What if the lift doesn't work again, and then we all

have to go home? Maybe if you leave Riverside Village, you can *never* get back to the present day! What if that's what happens to me? I'll be just like her. I'll have lost my life – not just a year, *two* years. I'll never really know what happened and never be happy again. I clench my hands into fists; they're clammy and slippy with fear.

'This is nice, isn't it?' Mum smiles at me. 'The four of us out like this?'

I nod, gulping hard. 'Mm,' I say, trying to twist my face into a smile.

I spend the rest of the morning following the others around in a daze, trying to act normal, trying not to count the seconds till we're back and I can find out what's happened to Autumn.

Come on, please let's just go back, I say in my mind, over and over again. *Please let everything be OK.*

The second Mum pulls into the car park, I throw my door open.

'Steady on, Jen, I've not even turned the engine off.'

'How come Jenni never gets told off properly?' Craig moans. I pinch his leg as I jump out of the car.

'I'll be back soon,' I say. 'I've just got to check something.'

I run round to Autumn's block. As I approach her apartment – the new one on the ground floor – the door opens and Autumn's dad appears.

'Hey Jenni,' he says. He looks as though he's lost a load of weight, and his hair's grey, but other than that he looks normal. He even smiles at me.

'Hi, Mr Leonard,' I say nervously. *Is he off to the pub?*

He picks up an easel and a box of paints by the side of the door. 'Just off to hang out in the woods for some inspiration,' he says. 'I thought this would be an appropriate place to get started again. Wish me luck.' Then he gestures inside. 'She's in there with her mum,' he says. 'See you later.'

I go inside and stop in the hallway. 'Hello?' My hands are sweating. What am I going to find here this time?

'In here,' Mrs Leonard shouts back from the living room.

She's plonking a pile of clothes down on the sofa and opening up an ironing board. 'I just spotted this in a cupboard and thought I'd do a bit of ironing,' she says. 'I can't remember the last time I bothered.'

Nor can I. I think the Leonards used to have a cleaner who did things like that. Autumn's mum was always far too glamorous to do *ironing*!

She plugs in the iron and switches it on. 'She's in her room,' she says. 'Go on in. I think you're just the tonic she needs today.'

'Today?' I ask. 'Why today?'

Mrs Leonard rolls her eyes. 'She's having one of those days. Good job you're here. You deal with them much better than I do.'

Then she goes back to the pile of clothes and I make my way to Autumn's bedroom. *Those days? What days?*

What am I going to face on the other side of this door?

I knock on the door. No reply.

'Autumn?' I push the door open. She's inside. She's sitting on her bed, facing away from me.

'How come you didn't answer?' I ask, trying to keep my voice light, despite the quiver I can feel behind it.

She shrugs.

'Autumn?' I cross the room and stand in front of her. She looks so different. Her face is pale and lean; her lovely red hair is lank and lifeless; even more so than last time. She looks about ten years older than she is – unless I've gone even further forward than I thought.

She looks up at me. 'What are you doing in those old clothes?' she asks.

I look down at myself and feel ridiculous. To Autumn, I'm wearing clothes that are two years out of date. 'I don't know,' I say. I try to sound cheerful. 'Anyway, I haven't come round here to talk about my clothes!'

'What *have* you come round for?' she asks sullenly.

'I've come round to see you!' I say. 'I didn't realise I had to have a reason!'

'*Everything* has a reason,' Autumn says. Then in a bitter aside, she adds, 'Apparently.'

'What d'you mean?' I ask, sitting on the bed next to her.

Autumn shrugs again. 'It doesn't matter.'

'It does matter. Tell me.'

Autumn lets out a heavy breath. 'Just something I read in one of Mum's millions of self-help books.'

The thought of Autumn's mum reading self-help books is so far from reality that if it wasn't for the fact that I no longer have any idea what reality is, I would burst out laughing on the spot. But one look at Autumn's face and laughter is a million light years away from my thoughts. Her eyes are red, her cheeks are hollow – her whole face looks about as empty as her voice sounds.

'All this. Mum keeps saying there must be a reason for it. As though Mikey being in that hospital bed for the last two years is some kind of test for the family – and she's determined to pass it.'

'They both seem to be coping better this – ' I nearly say 'this year' but stop myself. In Autumn's world, I've spent the last year in her life. I should know what's been going on. But how am I meant to find out without trying to tell her what's really going on with me? I don't think she's got it in her to believe me. Why would she? I can still hardly believe it, myself. 'Better than they have been,' I say eventually.

'I know, it's mad isn't it? It's been nearly two months and they're still determined to hold on to it.'

'Two months? Two months since what?' *What else has happened?*

'You know, the whole thing with his eyes.'

'Thing with his eyes?' I ask before I can stop myself.

Autumn looks at me. 'Opening them in the day and closing them at night.'

Can people do that when they're in a coma? Does this mean he's getting better?

154

Autumn goes on before I can even work out how to respond. 'Four times he did it – that was all. Even then, the doctors told us it didn't mean anything. Just a reflex, nothing to do with an improvement in his condition. And I don't know how many times they've told us since. But Mum and Dad don't hear that. All they can think of is that he opened his eyes. They're convinced it must mean something. They're determined to believe it's only a matter of time. Any day now we're going to be jumping around playing happy families again.'

Autumn's voice is so brittle it almost seems to crack the words as she speaks them.

'But that's not a bad thing, is it?' I ask as gently as I can. 'It's good to have some hope, isn't it?'

Autumn snorts, then shakes her head. 'You're as bad as them if you think that.'

'Why?'

'It's make-believe,' she snaps. 'Childish, unrealistic nonsense that everyone goes round telling themselves, just to make themselves feel better. And it's pointless, idiotic and stupid.'

I'm so thrown by Autumn's outburst that I not only don't know how to respond. I don't know what to do at all. I'm aware that I'm staring at her with my mouth wide open. I feel as though she's just fired a load of bullets right at my face. Where did all this anger come from?

'I'm sick of everyone pretending it's all going to be OK. I'm *sick* of it. Don't you understand?'

How am I meant to understand? I don't understand

what's happening to my own life. How can I begin to understand what's going on in *hers*?

'Autumn, I don't know what's been happening here,' I say.

'What, you mean you haven't actually been with me the whole of the last two years, and seen my parents gradually convince themselves everything's going to be fine – when it clearly *isn't*?

'Actually, that's exactly what I'm telling you,' I say. 'I haven't been here. I don't know about any of this!' I can feel myself getting cross, too. It's not fair for her to be getting so angry with me. I don't know what's going on! I need to tell her the truth. This is me and Autumn. We tell each other *everything*. Anyway, what have I got to lose?

'Look, do you remember me telling you about losing a year?' I say.

'Hm, let me think. You mean do I remember you trying to make an idiot of me this time last year?' she snaps. 'Yes, thank you. And in case you're thinking of trying again, don't waste your time; I'm not interested.'

'I'm not making an idiot of you; it was all true!'

'Sure it was. Oh, look.' Autumn points out of the window. 'See that pig flying through the air?'

She has to believe me. I can't stand being in this without her any more.

'I know how it happened,' I say, ignoring her sarcasm. 'It's the lift. It took me forward a year in time, to the exact same week a year ahead. Week 35, same date, same time of the day. It doesn't just take me up a floor.

156

I went to the *second* floor this time, and I've gone forward *two* years!'

Autumn stares at me as though I'm a piece of rubbish that's got in her way. 'Have you finished?'

Please Autumn. It's me, Jenni – your best friend! I wouldn't joke about something like this. 'You've got to believe me!'

'I've got to, have I? And who exactly says I've got to, if you don't mind telling me? I don't recall needing your permission for anything I decide to do.'

'Autumn, I . . . ' My words trail away and dissolve. It's useless. One look at her face is enough to tell me she's not interested in what I've got to say, even though it's the truth. I shake my head. 'Forget it.'

I start to walk away, but I stop at the door. What did Mrs Smith say, about how she found out the things that had happened, the things she'd missed? Ask the right questions, in the right way, and people will tell you everything you need to know. She's right. I have to try harder. I'm not going to just sit back and let all of this happen. The old Jenni might have done, but too much has changed, and I've changed with it. I need to try again.

'I don't want to fall out with you,' I say. Autumn's still looking at me with cold eyes, her arms crossed tightly over her chest. 'What's happened to you?' I ask. 'What's happened to us? This isn't us.'

She looks away.

'You're not even going to answer me?'

'I don't want to fall out with you either,' she says finally, her voice softening slightly.

'Then let's not,' I say, sitting back down next to her and reaching out to touch her arm. 'We're in this together,' I say. 'You're my best friend.'

Autumn leans her head against my shoulder and we sit in silence for a while. It's only when I realise that my shoulder is damp that I see she's crying.

'Autumn, what is it?' I ask.

'I just – I just – I don't know how to cope with it all,' she gasps, her words bumping out in big sobs. 'Everyone else is getting their lives together, and it's only now that mine feels like it's falling apart.'

'What d'you mean? Why is your life falling apart?'

Autumn shakes her head and wipes her palm across her eyes. 'I can't – I can't stop seeing it,' she says eventually.

'Seeing what?'

'Mikey,' she says in a whisper. 'I dream about the accident every night, and all day he's there in my mind, in his bed. Not moving. He's never going to move again, never going to see me, talk to me. I can't bear it, Jen.'

I wrap my arms around her. 'Don't say that.'

Autumn pushes away from me. 'Don't say what – the truth?' she says, her voice suddenly harsh again. 'Oh, you're just as bad as them. Why don't you go and talk to my mum instead? You can play pretend together. She can tell you about the miraculous recovery Mikey's going to make and you can tell her all about your time machine.'

She gets up and stands at the window, arms folded,

facing away from me. 'What do you think it's like knowing that you've ruined your whole family's lives?' she says eventually.

'What? But it wasn't your fault!'

'Oh, really?' Autumn picks up a brush and starts pulling it through her hair. 'Like I said, why don't you go and swap pretend stories with my mum? I wouldn't blame you for wanting to spend time with anyone else – why would you want to be with me?'

I stand up and join her at the window, standing in front of her so she has to look at me. 'Autumn,' I say gently.

'What?'

'I don't believe I'd ever want to spend time with any-one as much as I want to be with you.'

Another yank of the brush through her lank hair. 'Whatever.'

'Maybe it's you who doesn't want to be with me. Maybe you're pushing *me* away.'

'How do you work that one out?'

'I dunno. Maybe you want to prove to yourself that no one wants to be around you.'

'And why would I want to do that?'

'I don't know. Maybe because you blame yourself for what happened to Mikey, and it's made you think you're such a bad person that no one would want to be with you – and no one can reject you if you reject them first?' I bite into my lip while I wait for her to answer. I've put my finger on it! Maybe I can fix this, get our friendship back on track, mend the whole—

'Well, thanks for your insights, Sigmund Freud,' Autumn snaps. 'But if I wanted to listen to home-made therapy jargon, I'd go to your mum.' She turns her back on me again. 'Now if you don't mind, I think I'd rather you left me in peace.'

'Autumn!' I follow her to her dressing table and reach out to touch her arm. She snatches it away. 'I don't understand why you're being like this. It feels like you hate me.'

'You really want me to explain?'

'Yes,' I say, my voice quivering.

She finally turns round to face me, looks flatly into my eyes. 'Because you let me down, Jenni. Because you didn't show up. Because I couldn't find you anywhere so I made Mum take me without you. Because we'd booked two horses, so Mikey came too. Because your mum didn't turn up, and the ambulance didn't turn up – and the delays meant that it was too late to do any-thing. Because – ' She stops suddenly.

'Because what?' My voice is a hoarse whisper.

Autumn's eyes are shining as she looks deep into mine. 'Because it happened to *my* brother,' she says finally, 'not yours.'

I open my mouth to reply. Nothing comes out.

'You asked,' she says flatly. 'And that's your answer. That what you wanted to hear?'

I swallow hard. I still don't even know why I didn't turn up. Maybe it was because I'd gone forward in time and the old Jenni disappeared. Maybe it was something else altogether. I'll probably never know, but it doesn't matter anyway. The fact is, I wasn't there and they went without me. Was this whole thing my fault?

'No, I thought not,' she says. 'Now do you understand?'

I find my voice. 'I think so. You blame me for it happening, and you wish it had happened to my brother instead of yours. I should think that's normal, a natural kind of – '

'Oh for heaven's sake Jenni, can't you stop being so flipping *reasonable*?' she bursts out. 'It's me, OK! You were right. It's *me* who pushed you away, *me* who wouldn't see *you*. Me who can't forgive *anyone* for what happened – you, Mum, Dad – and yes, all right, myself! OK? I can't forgive myself.' Autumn stops as a sob chokes into her voice.

'Forgive yourself?' I reach out to put my hand on her arm. She doesn't snatch it away. 'There's nothing to forgive.'

'You don't understand,' she croaks.

'What?' I ask softly. 'What don't I understand?'

'I egged him on. I made him gallop. He was really nervous, but I said he could do it. I teased him, called him a wimp. So he did it – he galloped – and he was thrown off. And then I thought he was all right. I didn't insist on getting him to hospital straight away. I believed him when he said he was fine. It was *my* fault. Everyone else is dealing with it now. You're OK. Mum and Dad are OK. Everyone's getting on with their lives – and I'm stuck here in this nightmare that I can't stop reliving. Don't you get it?'

'Get what?'

'I hate *everyone* for what happened!' she cries. 'I hate everyone for moving on. And I know how unfair that is. But this anger – I can't get rid of it; I can't get it out of me. I'm so filled with it and there's nothing I can do with it that's reasonable. So there's only one person left to hate. Only one person whose life I can ruin without having to feel even more guilty.' She turns her tear-stained face towards me.

'Yours,' I say blankly.

'Correct. Top marks.' She rubs her palm fiercely across her eyes. 'Want a prize for that?'

I pull my hand away from her arm. 'Why are you being so mean?'

'I've just told you, haven't I? I thought you were meant to understand, meant to be a good listener like your mum. Funny how wrong you can be about people, isn't it? She turned out not to be so great, too.'

'What do you mean by that?' I snap. I can't help it. If she wants to push me away, fine. Let her. But I'm not going to lie down like a doormat just so she can stamp on me – and my mum.

'Driving your dad away like that.'

I clutch my stomach. For a moment, I actually think she's thumped me – but she's not standing near enough, so I know it was only words. 'How dare you?' I whisper eventually.

I can't say anything else. My throat is too choked up. Autumn pulls at her hair, for a second looking guilty, maybe even ashamed. Maybe she knows she's gone too far.

'My mum hasn't driven anyone away. They're just having a break. It's a trial. They'll get back together,' I say woodenly.

'Yeah, right.' Autumn shakes her head. 'When are you going to stop living in cloud cuckoo land, Jen? Hey, maybe *that's* where you've been for the last two years – while you've been pretending you've not been on planet earth?'

'I can't believe you're being like this,' I say. 'I want to help you. I'm trying to be nice and all you can do is—'

'Oh, lucky me. You've come round to be *nice*. Well guess what? I don't *need* your help! In fact, I don't need you at all!'

'I – ' I back away to the door, and then I stop. What's *happening*? Autumn and I have never done this before. I mean, she can be a bit hot-headed at times, and we have argued over silly things, but we always make up two minutes later. Not this time, though. This feels very different. 'I can't handle this, Autumn,' I say, opening the door. 'Not on top of everything else. I'm sorry.'

'That's right!' she calls after me. 'Just walk away from me. Can't hack it, can you? Can't deal with the facts, with *me*. Well, you're doing me a favour! I don't want you hanging around the place any more. It's finished, Jenni. Our friendship. Over, OK? Can you get that into your thick head? I don't want you hanging round me any more. Ever!'

'Fine!' I yell back, my patience running out at last. 'You want to cut me out of your life? Go ahead. Think I care? Well I don't!' I know I don't mean it, and I wish I could snatch the words back – but my voice is tied up in knots, somewhere deep inside my chest.

Autumn looks at me, her face still and hard. 'Well, that's that settled then,' she says calmly. 'Have a nice life.' She follows me to the door, and slams it shut behind me.

As soon as I've left the apartment, I burst into tears. I can't help it. I just can't believe how awful things have turned out. I thought it was bad enough the first time I went forward. This is getting worse and worse.

I head for the lift. I need to get back to the present day. I've got to get out of this nightmare. I know that all that's waiting for me is another nightmare, but at least it's one that doesn't have years of history I don't know about heaped on top of it.

I climb the stairs up to the second floor so I can get the lift back down. But I stop at the top of the stairs.

If I go back, I'll *never* know how things turn out. All I'll be able to do is watch these horrible events unfold, day by day. I can't help wondering where all of this is going to end up. Will I ruin my life like Mrs Smith did? I feel in my pocket for her letter – a reminder of how badly my life could go wrong if I don't do something about it – and a reminder that I've promised myself I want to somehow find a way to help her too.

What's to become of all of this? All of us? I'm about to take the letter out of my pocket and read it, when I have a better idea. The letter can wait a bit longer.

There were three floors in the lift. I've only been to two, so far.

I've got one more chance to find out how the future's going to turn out. One more chance to convince myself it'll all be OK in the end.

I have to know.

I gasp out loud when I see the lift. It's been cordoned off, sealed with layers of yellow tape, criss-crossing all the way from the floor to the ceiling. I came out in such a hurry earlier, I didn't even turn round to look at it. *When did they do that?*

I quickly look over my shoulder. There's no one around. My heart's trying to leap out of my chest. I've *got* to find out. I've got to know it's all going to be all right at some point.

But what if it isn't? a nagging voice in my head asks. *What if my life just gets worse and worse and worse?*

Either way, isn't it better to know? At least I can prepare myself if I know what's coming.

Another quick look round, and then I tear at the tape, pulling and ripping it off just enough so I can get at the door and press the 'call' button.

Nothing happens. Silence. I rest my head against the door. *Please work, please work.* I bang my fist on the door out of frustration. *What am I going to do?*

And then. A clunking noise, from deep inside the building, cranking upwards, whirring slowly towards me. I jump backwards as the noise comes closer, and then I pull open the door and drag the gate across.

With the briefest of pauses, I nod to myself. *Come on.* I shut both doors and eye the buttons, staring at them as though they're the enemy.

And then I press *3*. The lift seems to take forever to go up one floor. Scraping and squeaking, it grinds slowly upwards, jumping to a stop with a thud that makes my teeth rattle. How much more of this will it let me do? It seems to be falling apart more and more every time I use it.

The moment I step out of the lift, there's a crashing noise behind me. It sounds like a clap of thunder or a collapsing building. Instinctively, I hurl myself against the opposite wall, crouching into a tight ball.

But when I open my eyes, there's nothing. Silence. No sign of destruction, or yellow tape or anything. *What on earth . . . ?*

It can't be! The lift – it's disappeared!

I scramble back to where it should be. It's completely gone! Now there's just a blank white wall in place of the old steel doors.

I scratch at the wall, pummelling it with my fists. *What am I going to do?* There's no lift. I'll be trapped here forever!

How could I have been so stupid? So determined to find things out that I didn't need to know. How could I have thought this would make things any better? Why did I throw away my chance simply to go back and get on with things?

I've lost three years of my life and I'll *never* get them back.

11

I stumble out of the building and glance around. Everything looks different, yet again.

Was that shed always there? Did it used to be painted white? Has the hotel always had that extension? Did that lamp post always exist? Suddenly I'm doubting *everything*; everything I can see as well as everything that's happened to me since we got here. I feel as if I've just got off a roundabout that's been spinning too fast.

I look along the row of ground floor apartments. At least they look the same. Before I realise it, I'm standing outside Autumn's apartment, trying to gather my nerve. I need to see her. Whether I'm ever going to get back the years I've lost or not, the only thing I know is that I have to make things right with Autumn.

I keep lifting my hand to knock on the door, then thinking of a hundred reasons why it might not be a good idea. Will she even want to see me? Did we make up last year or have we argued again since then?

There's only one way to find out.

I step closer to the apartment. I'm about to knock when the door is thrown open – and Autumn is in front of me. Another year older, different again. Her hair looks more like the old Autumn's, a bit more lively, but her face is harder somehow, more set.

For a second, we stare at each other in silence. She's the first to speak. 'What are you doing here?' she says, looking at me as though I've just landed from Mars.

I open my mouth to reply.

'Who you talking to, Autumn?' Another voice comes from the hall before I have a chance to answer. A smiling face follows the voice, peeking round the door. 'You!' the voice says. It's Christine! A 15-year-old version of the girl Autumn always called Barbie One. What's Autumn doing with *her*?

'What are you doing here?' Christine asks, in an echo of Autumn's still unanswered question. Why are they both so shocked to see me at my best friend's apartment? *Surely* we made up after that awful row? Could it really have been so bad that I walked out of here and didn't come back till now? A year without Autumn? It's unthinkable.

'What's going on?' Someone else comes into the hallway, peering over Autumn's shoulder, before I manage to answer. It's Sally. Barbie Two. They're both plastered in bright eye shadow, hair tied into ridiculous shapes on top of their heads, and their designer gear on. What is Autumn *doing* with them? Half of me wants to laugh. The other half of me is staring at three cold faces waiting for me to explain myself.

'I've come to see Autumn,' I say firmly. I'm not going to let them see I'm nervous. I've nothing to lose any more. I've already lost three years of my life. Nothing they can do can hurt me – and I'm *not* going to lose Autumn. I won't let it happen. If I have to stay in this awful reality for the rest of my life then the least I can do is get my best friend back and live in it with her; I don't care what it takes.

Autumn's eyes open wide. 'What for?' she asks, staring at me in confusion.

'What for?' I repeat. 'I didn't know I had to have a reason.'

Autumn opens her mouth to speak, then glances at Sally before replying. I'm sure I see Sally give her a quick nod. Since when did Autumn need *Sally*'s permission to speak?

Sally decides to speak for her anyway. 'Well, I think you do, actually,' she says, 'after everything you've done.'

'Everything I've – Autumn, can I speak to you on your own?'

Autumn glances at Sally again. 'You can say what you have to say in front of my friends,' she says, as though she's incapable of talking to me without their approval. 'And make it quick,' she adds. 'We're going out.'

Christine folds her arms, standing possessively behind Autumn. 'This should be good,' she says.

For a second, I can feel the nerves flutter in my stomach, but I mentally bat them away. I'm not going to let anyone get in the way of my friendship with Autumn – certainly not the Barbies!

I clear my throat. 'Look, I don't know why you're so mad at me,' I begin.

Sally laughs out loud. 'She doesn't know why we're mad. She's even stupider than she looks.'

Autumn doesn't say anything. She's looking at me, waiting for me to carry on. Her eyes are heavy and sad. She doesn't look angry at all. In fact, she looks like someone I hardly know – someone who gives up, someone who lets other people talk for her, who doesn't have the energy to fight her own battles, who doesn't have any energy at all. That's not Autumn. Not the Autumn I know, anyway.

'I don't know what I've done,' I say. I think about what happened only minutes ago. It was the worst argument we've ever had. But that was a year ago in Autumn's life! She can't still be angry over that, can she?

This time Christine speaks. 'Oh, so she thinks not being there for someone for a year and then turning up on their doorstep is normal behaviour, does she?'

So it's true? We've not spoken for a year? I can hardly believe it – but I'm not going to let any of them see how sad they've made me feel. I need to take control of the situation, for Autumn's sake as much as mine. As if her life wasn't bad enough before, now she seems to have this pair of numbskulls permanently fixed to her sides!

And I wish they'd stop referring to me as 'she', as

though I'm not here. Why do they keep talking for Autumn, anyway?

'I don't care how long it's been,' I say. 'I'm here now, and that's what matters.' I look Autumn in the eyes and make myself speak as calmly as I can. 'Autumn, if I have let you down, if I haven't been there for you, if I've been a bad friend – I'm here to make amends. I'm sorry. I want to start again.'

Autumn holds my eyes for ages. It seems the rest of us are all holding our breath while we wait for her response.

'We don't need to listen to this,' Christine says eventually. Then she turns to Autumn. 'Come on, let's go.'

'Autumn, what do *you* think?' I insist. 'You haven't even answered me.' But she won't meet my eyes.

'Where are you going?' I ask as they push past me.

'Down to this cool place by the river,' Christine says casually.

They mean our place! Mine and Autumn's. I barge down the path after them. 'Autumn, that's *our* place!' I shout.

'Ahh, she thinks it's their place,' Sally smirks. 'How childish.' She stops and looks round at me. 'Almost as childish as those ridiculous clothes she's wearing.'

I look down at myself. My top that was perfectly acceptable this morning is stretched across a body that's three years older than I feel. My arms are bare from the elbows downwards and my jeans that were huge when I put them on now look like pedal pushers. All my new-found confidence disappears as I realise I probably look like an extra out of *Oliver*.

Christine and Sally are marching ahead with Autumn in between them. They're talking over her to each other. It's as though she's an object that they've been given the responsibility of looking after – not a person who they care about.

I run to catch up with them. I don't care what they say or how I look; they can't shake me off like a piece of unwanted rubbish.

'Autumn, let's make up,' I say, desperately trying to think of a way to end this nightmare. I can't bear the thought of being stuck in this awful world and not having Autumn by my side. 'I'm sorry, I'm sorry for everything I said, everything I did. Please.'

Autumn throws a quick look at me as Christine links her arm and practically pulls her down the road. For a moment, Autumn's face softens. She looks as though she might accept my apology. She opens her mouth to speak. Just then, Sally grabs Autumn's other arm and they march on together. Autumn looks as though she's being carted off by a couple of police officers.

'She doesn't need to be dragged along by the pair of you. She can walk on her own, you know!' I shout.

Autumn stops in her tracks and turns round. 'Don't tell Christine and Sally what to do,' she says, a flash of anger creeping into her sad eyes. 'They're just looking out for me. They're my friends, OK?'

I sigh as she looks away from me again, and traipse behind them like a stray dog following a stranger in the hope of finding a friend.

As we approach the bridge, a couple of older boys

are walking towards us. Christine and Sally nudge each other and flick their hair. 'Hi Darren, hi Paul,' they say in unison.

'Hi girls,' one of the boys says. He's tall and lanky with floppy blond hair and bright green eyes. The other one smiles at them. Both of them completely ignore Autumn and me.

'We're just taking our friend out for a walk.'

'Taking her for a walk? She's not a dog, you know!' I say, for the first time seeing the pair of us united against everyone else. A couple of puppies bouncing around just needing love and understanding. I will Autumn to look at me so we can grin at each other, knowing that we've had the same thought, as we always do.

She doesn't look at me. It hurts so much I almost cry out.

'Her brother's in a coma,' Christine says solemnly to the boys. She sounds proud of herself, as though she's showing them a medal on her collar. 'We're making sure she's OK.'

Autumn's face reddens but she doesn't say anything.

The taller boy nods approvingly. 'Good for you,' he says. Then he looks at Autumn for the first time. He gives her a kind of sympathetic look. 'Lucky you've got them, eh?'

'Yeah,' Autumn says without conviction.

The boys move on. 'See you later, girls.'

Christine and Sally giggle and talk in squeaky voices all the rest of the way to the bridge. I want to say something to Autumn but I don't know what, or how. Does she *really* not mind being talked about like that? As though she's some kind of charity case that makes others look good just for spending time with her? Where has all her fight gone, all her life?

When we get to our place by the river, Christine and Sally plonk themselves down on the grass and Autumn awkwardly sits down with them. I hover, standing on the outside of the little circle 'So, which one do you want?' Christine asks, with a girly giggle.

'Darren!' Sally says straight away.

'Good! I like Paul best! We could go out as a foursome.'

They break into huge giggles and I try to catch Autumn's eye so I can roll my eyes at her and so she can pull a face at me and make me laugh. Once more, she doesn't even look my way.

'What about Autumn?' I ask. 'Which one's she having?'

The Barbies both look at me as though I'm a fleck of dirt on a brand new designer outfit, and move on to the next subject. 'Who do you think's going to win Pop Star Sensations?' Sally asks.

'I love that Gary – he's got the cutest bum,' Christine replies. Then, as an afterthought, she turns to Autumn. 'Don't you think?'

Autumn swallows before replying. 'Yeah, really cute,' she says with a smile. But it's not the kind of smile I'm used to seeing from Autumn. It's false and forced. Two things Autumn doesn't do.

I don't even hear their reply. I tune out and stare at the river. All I can think is, *what on earth is she doing with these airheads?*

Sally looks round and yawns. 'I have to say, I'm not sure what's so great about it here. It's boring!' she says. 'Shall we go to the games room and see if any of the boys are in there?'

Boys again! Is that *all* she thinks about?

'We could skim some stones,' I say.

Christine looks at me with such a horrified expression on her face that for a moment I wonder if I've actually said, *Hey, I know, let's run around with nothing on and see if we can spot an alien.*

'I'll pass, thanks,' she says, waving a hand dismissively at me.

'Me too,' Sally adds.

'Autumn?' I ask. She looks at me. '*Please*,' I say, holding my breath as I silently beg her to leave this awful pair behind and join me by the river.

Autumn looks at the Barbies and then at me. Then she drags herself up. 'OK,' she says heavily. 'Might as well.' I only just manage to stop myself from grabbing her in a tight hug.

We head over to the water's edge and pick up a few stones. I throw one across the water and it plops in after one bounce. Autumn throws hers in and it skims the surface beautifully, bouncing on the river six times before slicing into the water.

'Not lost your touch, then,' I say, attempting a smile.

Autumn picks up another stone and doesn't reply.

'How can you do this?' I ask.

'Do what?'

'Hang out with *them*?'

Autumn shrugs. 'They take my mind off things,' she says. 'It's better than hanging out on my own.'

I want to tell her she doesn't ever need to be on her own – she's got me! But after last time, I know better than to come out with statements that probably don't match her reality, even if they're part of the bedrock of mine.

And I want to tell her about all the snide looks I've noticed Christine and Sally passing. I'm sure they're whispering about us now, in fact. But I don't want to do anything to give Autumn an excuse to have a go at me.

'I still don't get how you can you bear to be with them,' I say in the end. 'They're so superficial; they're like plastic dolls! They don't care about you.'

'Maybe superficial is exactly what I want right now,' Autumn says lifelessly. 'If you don't talk about anything that matters, no one can say anything that'll hurt you – and you don't have to talk about the things that are eating away at you from the inside.'

I decide not to push it.

'And anyway, who says they don't care about me?' Autumn goes on. 'Why would they hang out with me if they didn't care?'

I shrug, thinking back to the incident with the two boys. 'Maybe they want to look good or something. Show off to boys about how sensitive and thoughtful they are.'

Autumn turns to me. 'Are you trying to make me feel better?' she asks, 'because if you are, you're not making a very good job of it.'

'I'm sorry. I just don't trust them, and I don't like them,' I say. 'And I thought you felt the same way.'

Autumn talks to the ground. 'Yeah, well my choices got a bit more limited.'

I don't know how to reply. I don't know how we got to this point. All I know is we had an awful argument – a year ago. Is that the last time we spoke?

'Autumn, how did we get to this?' I ask carefully.

'Get to what?'

'This. Not being friends. You're my best friend, the best friend anyone could want in the whole world. I'm sorry about what I said before.'

'Before?'

'I mean – last year,' I correct myself, feeling ridiculous referring to something that's only just happened as last year. 'Is that what this is about?'

Autumn breathes out heavily. 'What else is it going to be about?' she asks.

'So that's the last time we spoke?' I hold my breath while I wait for her to answer.

'You lost your memory now?' she says. 'Or perhaps you've just lost another year and gone forward in time again!' She stares at me with a challenge in her eyes. For the first time, there's a hint of life on her face. Is she asking me to tell her the truth or warning me not to even try it? I daren't risk it again – not when we're actually communicating. I look down and don't say anything.

'Anyway, you know we've talked since then,' Autumn goes on. 'But it's always ended up the same way, so

I'm glad we gave up trying. It was too painful.'

'I don't want us to fall out,' I say. 'I never want that.'

'Too late, Jen. Already happened.'

'You seem to hate me,' I say. 'I don't understand why.'

'I don't hate you at all,' Autumn says. 'I just can't be around you. Being with Sally and Christine takes me away from it all. Being with you just reminds me how much it all hurts.'

'And that's why you've pushed me away for the last year.'

Autumn shrugs.

As we sit in silence, I try to get my head round what's happening. Try to believe it could really be true. Two days ago we'd both just arrived at Riverside Village. We hugged each other as soon as we met up in the car park; we gossiped right here by the river; we wanted to spend every minute together. She was smiling. Always smiling. This isn't Autumn. Something has gone horribly, horribly wrong.

'I wish it wasn't like this,' I say eventually.

'Yeah, me too,' Autumn replies wistfully. 'But it is. I can't change what happened. No one can. And you know the worst thing?'

'What?'

Autumn pauses for ages. Then almost in a whisper, she says, 'I haven't got anyone to talk to about . . . ' She stops, swallows hard, then shakes her head. 'Forget it,' she says.

'About what?'

She turns away and swipes her palm across her eyes. 'Nothing.'

'Look I know how hard it's all been for you. I understand – '

'You *don't* know, Jen! You *don't* understand!' Autumn bursts out. 'That's just it. *No one* understands. You don't get it at *all*.'

'What don't I get?'

'How I feel. What it's like to be me, to have lived my life for the last three years. Was it *you* who sat by your little brother's side, holding his hand so long you couldn't feel your fingers any more, too scared to let go or fall asleep in case he wasn't there when you woke up? Was it *you* who sat there while a surgeon walked into the room and calmly told your parents that your brother had an internal bleed in his head that had spread too far for them to fix because he wasn't brought to the hospital in time? Was it you who had to hear the words that would break your family into pieces – that your little brother had slipped into a coma and would almost certainly never come out of it?'

I stare at Autumn. I want to hug her, but the person in front of me looks so brittle that if I did, I feel as if it might break her in half. Not that she'd even let me, anyway.

'Three years ago,' She looks at her watch. 'A couple of hours from now, when the surgeon told us about Mikey. Two pm on the dot. Exactly a day after the accident, my family's world fell apart. You gained a little sister on the same day as I lost my little brother.'

'You didn't lose – '

'As good as,' Autumn says before I can finish my sentence.

I bite my cheek.

'And now it's too late to do anything.'

'What do you mean it's too late?' I ask.

Autumn shakes her head. 'Forget it. Just don't say you know how hard it's been. OK?' She drops the stones she was holding in her hands and goes over to the others. 'Are we going back?' she says to them. 'I've had enough of it round here.'

Sally and Christine get up. 'Yeah, come on, let's go back to mine,' Sally says. 'I'll paint your nails and do your hair up, and then we can go to the games room and see who's there.'

'Fine. Whatever. Just let's go,' Autumn says, and walks off. Christine and Sally trail behind, giggling and gossiping all the way.

I run to catch up with Autumn. 'Autumn. Come on – do your hair up? Paint your nails? Going to the games room to check out the boys? That's not the Autumn I know!'

'Look, you're right – I don't want to do those things. It's not me, it's not what I want. OK? Happy? But how can I tell them that? Jenni, don't you see? I'm *not* the Autumn you know any more. That's the whole point. I hardly know *who* I am any more. I know they treat me like an idiot most of the time, and I couldn't care less about the silly things they talk about – but what options do I have? I just don't have the strength to tell them to get lost.'

You've got me, I want to say. *I can be strong enough for us both, if that's what you need.* I keep my mouth shut though. I don't want to start another argument.

'And you know what else?' Autumn goes on. 'You're not the Jen I thought I knew any more, either.'

I look at her for a long time. 'No, I'm not,' I say eventually. 'And d'you know what? It's time I proved it. It's time someone stood up for *both* of us.'

I turn round and wait for the Barbies to catch up. 'Hey, guess what?' I say. 'Autumn doesn't want to come round to yours. She's not interested in checking out boys who only talk to you because they think you're so kind looking after your poor bereaved friend. And she doesn't need you to do anything to her hair or her nails. She's fine as she is. Oh, and she couldn't give two hoots about Pop Star Sensation – and she doesn't even *know* who Gary is, let alone care! So you can keep your stupid, superficial world, and you can forget the *"Oh we're so kind, we look after the girl whose brother's in a coma"* goodie-goodie-two-shoes act, because she's not buying it any more – and nor am I!'

The three of them stare at me. For a moment, I think I've gone too far. But Christine and Sally have turned so red I know I've hit the nail on the head.

Christine flicks her head back. 'Don't you start—'

'Yes I will start!' I cut her off. 'And I'll finish.' I glance at Autumn. She's staring at me, mouth open, eyes wide. Should I stop? There's something in Autumn's eyes that I don't recognise. Then I realise what it is: admiration, gratitude, even relief. That's all I need to spur me on.

I turn back to Christine and Sally. 'You aren't real friends,' I say. 'You don't truly care about Autumn. You only ever wanted to be with her because she was popular and you thought it'd make you look good to be seen with her, and now you just want to be seen to be caring so you can get noticed by a couple of stupid boys.'

Sally steps forward. 'Now hang on a minute—'

'No I won't hang on a minute!' I say, fury and loyalty pushing me on. Someone has to say this – and that someone is going to have to be me. This whole stupid, awful reality has taken so much away from me that I haven't got anything to lose any more, so I'm going to tell it how it is.

'Autumn's not a badge for you to parade around with so you can pick up brownie points. She's a person – a fantastic person. She's the best friend anyone could want and if you don't realise that, then you're even more dumb than I thought!'

Before they have a chance to answer, I turn and stomp back to Autumn. She's gawping at me. 'I'm sorry,' I say. 'I don't want to ruin any of your friendships, and if they truly matter to you then I'll apologise to them, once I've calmed down. But I had to do that. I'm not going to sit and watch this joke any more. You matter too much to me for that.'

Autumn swallows, looking across at Christine and Sally. She doesn't say anything.

'Listen. I don't want us to fall out. I *never* want us to fall out,' I say. 'If you feel the same way, come round to mine later.'

Autumn still doesn't answer.

'If you don't come, I'll know you don't want us to be friends and I'll leave you alone. I won't bother you again.'

Eventually, she nods.

'OK,' I say awkwardly. 'I'll leave it with you.' Then I turn and walk away, heading back to my apartment and suddenly realising yet again that I haven't got a clue what's waiting for me when I get there. All I know is that I need to get back to my own territory and find something I can recognise – something that will help me find my way through this crazy, awful world that I've landed in.

I need a place where I can think. I need to be on my own. I need to make a plan.

12

'That you, Jen?' a woman's voice calls as I close the front door behind me.

I step into the living room. There's a strange woman sitting on the sofa with Dad. 'Who are you?' I ask.

Dad puts his paper down. 'Jenni. Don't be so rude.'

The woman puts her hand on his arm. 'It's all right, darling. I don't mind.'

'Well, I do,' he says. 'Jenni, apologise to Karen now.'

I stare at them both: Dad's face dark and angry. The strange woman – Karen, apparently – smiling at me through big brown eyes. 'She doesn't have to apologise,' she says. 'We're all right aren't we, Jen?'

'I don't know who you are,' I say before I can stop myself.

Karen-apparently sucks in her breath as she half closes her eyes. Then she smiles again. 'I'll make a cup of tea,' she says, leaning forward to get up.

Dad stops her. 'No you won't,' he says firmly. 'Not

until Jenni apologises.' He turns back to me. 'We talked this through. We've all had plenty of time to get used to it, and if Craig can accept Karen then I think you jolly well can do, too.'

My brain tries to do a quick catch-up on three years' worth of missing facts. *Come on, Jenni. Remember you're fifteen now. Everyone else's world has moved on three years. Get with it!*

'I'm sorry, Karen,' I say, trying to get my voice to come out sounding natural. 'It was just a shock. I just need to get used to it.'

'Get used to it?' Dad repeats. 'You've had six months! We talked about Karen coming with us. You said you didn't mind.'

Six months?

Karen gets up. 'I'm going to get that cuppa,' she says, lightly touching my arm as she passes me.

'I thought you liked Karen,' Dad says in a lower voice. 'I thought you got on well.'

'I – I . . .' *Say the right things. Act as if you know what's going on.* 'I do,' I say eventually. I suppose it's not Dad's fault that as far as I'm concerned, he and Mum were still together yesterday. In my world. In my messed up, impossible world.

'Well, do you think you could act like you do, please?' Dad says sternly. Then his voice softens a little. 'We've talked about it so much. I know it's hard for you – it's hard for me too, sometimes. You know I'll always love your mum, and it would have been brilliant if we could have made it work. But we didn't – and we're both happy with how things are now. We're happy enough. Can't that be enough for you, too?'

I nod. My head is swimming.

'Thank you.' Dad picks up his paper again. 'We're having lunch soon, all right? Try to be civil.'

'I will,' I reply. 'Where's Craig?'

'Out with his pals. He'll be back soon.'

'Where's Thea?' I ask, suddenly remembering I have a baby sister now.

Dad shoots me a filthy look.

'What?' I ask.

'You know very well that Thea's with your mum. Jenni, please stop trying to make this hard for us.'

'I'm not trying –' I let out a heavy breath. 'Forget it,' I say. 'I'm going to my room.'

I go to the room I share with Craig and slump down on my bed. His side is a complete mess. Dirty khaki trousers, inside-out jeans and crumpled up t-shirts litter the floor. There are no teddies on his pillow this year. There's a chemistry set on the floor by his bed.

My side is tidy, the bed made, clothes put away. I sit up and look around. Maybe there'll be a clue somewhere. Something that can help all of this to make sense, to fit together. Better still – something that could help me work out how to get back. I feel as though I'm doing a jigsaw; the only problem is that the pieces are from three different puzzles and they're all mixed up together.

I scavenge through the bits and pieces on the dressing table. Most of it's Craig's. Miniature cars broken into pieces with their wheels hanging off, a penknife, screwed up tissues and bits of paper, a magnifying glass. My side just has a few things on it: a bottle of perfume, two necklaces, some mascara. Mascara! I can't imagine wearing make-up. Dad's always had this thing about me being too young, despite the fact that half the girls in my year already go to school looking like models. I've only ever put make-up on round at Autumn's when I've been staying over so Dad doesn't have to realise his little baby's growing up.

No clues. Nothing to help me work out how to play this new game called my life.

I turn back to the bed and glance at the bedside table. Maybe there'll be something in there. I yank the drawer open. There's a book. I pull it out. Of course – my diary! I scan through the pages for the latest entry. It's dated last Saturday.

I hope Autumn's coming to the timeshare this week. I wish we could go back to how we were. Maybe over there we'll be able to try again. Maybe this time it won't end up in a huge row. I just don't know how to talk to her any more. It seems there's nothing I can do that doesn't create an argument. Maybe she's right and we should just stop trying – but I can't. I want her back.

It was awful last Saturday at the disco. For once, I was out with Natalie and the others, making a reasonably good attempt at having fun. I'd almost forgotten how miserable this last year has been, but Autumn's face when she saw me there – it was so horrible. She looked at me as though I was a rodent that had crawled out of the drains. It was as if I had no right to be somewhere that she wanted to be. As if we hadn't shared everything in our lives like twins up until the last few years. Natalie said it's best to leave her. It probably is, but – oh, I don't know. I just miss her so much.

I wish I could have my life back how it used to be. Nothing's the same. Nothing will ever be the same again.

I wish I'd never gone in that stupid lift.

At least I've got the letter. No one knows about that. I know I'll find Mrs Smith again one day – and maybe then we can help each other out of this mess. Maybe if I can help her to be happy, this can all be different. If I could just do one thing right.

The letter! Of course! I've been so wrapped up with everything to do with Autumn that I'd forgotten all about it! I still don't even know what it says.

I reach into my pocket, pull out the pages and open them up.

Dear Bobby,
    I don't know if you will remember me. In fact, I very much doubt it. I

189

am the girl you spent carefree days with, and exchanged childish dreams with, many eons ago.

We spent a week of each year together - at the Riverside Hotel - and I have to tell you, those weeks were amongst the happiest of my life.

Whether you remember those days or not, I wanted to tell you - I have never forgotten them.

In fact, in recent years, the memories have played with me and the promises have plagued me. Do you remember our promises?

I should tell you first of all: I have lived a happy enough life. At least, as happy as it could have been, given my rather unusual circumstances. But more of that later. For now, I want to tell you this, and if it seems somewhat dramatic or obtuse, then at least I don't need to worry about what your reaction may be. I can tell you my true feelings - I can tell you anything at all - because I know that you will never read this letter. And so I am going to tell you the truth - the truth that I have never spoken aloud, and that no one has ever known. The secret that has *been stored in my heart, like a genie hidden in a bottle.*

My secret is that I have always loved you and I always will.

There, I've said it. And it's true. But it's also pointless, and so I am writing this letter to get the feelings out of me and let them rest, before they can take away any more of my years or trap me any longer with the hold they have over me. And so, Bobby, I –

The front door slams. 'Back!' a boy's voice shouts. Craig. A moment later, his feet thump up the stairs and I quickly fold the letter and shove it back in my pocket.

Craig appears at the door. A grown boy, mucky-faced, mud all over his t-shirt, spiky, gelled hair, childish scowl on his face. 'What you doing?' he asks in a grown-up, serious voice.

I get off the bed and pick up some of his clothes. 'Tidying.'

He shrugs. Then he squints at me. 'What are you *wearing*?'

I pull at my t-shirt. 'I—'

'Lunchtime!' Dad calls from the living room. 'Craig, get changed.'

Craig pulls a clean top out of the wardrobe and disappears into the bathroom. Shutting the bedroom door after him, I grab some clothes out of my ward-robe and throw them on. At least I *look* more normal now, even if I don't feel it.

We're just finishing lunch when there's a quiet knock at the door.

'I'll get it.' Craig leaps up from the table.

A moment later, he calls me from the hall. 'It's Autumn,' he says as he sits back down at the table.

'Autumn?' Dad looks surprised. 'I thought you two had fallen out.'

'We – we have. We had,' I mumble as I get up from the table.

'Have you made up again, then?'

'Um. I'm not sure. I think so, maybe,' I falter.

'Well, that's nice isn't it?' Dad says, smiling at Karen.

'OK if I go out?' I ask.

'Course it is, love.' Karen answers this time, putting a hand on Dad's knee. It feels really weird to see her do that.

'Great.' I hurry to the door.

Autumn's waiting outside. She gives me a shy smile as I close the door behind me and follow her out. 'Shall we go for a walk?' she asks.

'Definitely!' We walk along in silence for a while, following the path upriver, the opposite way from earlier.

'Look I'm sorry about before,' I say eventually. 'I shouldn't have gone off on one like that. I don't know what came over me.'

'Nor do I,' Autumn laughs.

I grimace. 'I shouldn't have done it,' I repeat.

Autumn reaches out to grab my arm. I stop walking. 'Yes, you should,' she says seriously. 'It was brilliant. It was like an electric shock.'

'What d'you mean?'

Autumn shakes her head. 'I don't know. I feel like you woke me up again. Seeing you like that. You've never done anything like that. It was always me, wasn't it? I'd always take the lead. I'd be the stroppy one, telling everyone else what to do.'

'Yeah, you could say that,' I say, a smile creeping in to the sides of my mouth.

'I always used to wish I could be more like you.'

I nearly fall over in shock. 'More like me?' I gasp. 'Why on earth would you want to be like *me*?'

Autumn kicks her feet in the gravel as she carries on up the path. 'You're so calm and steady. You take things as they come, take people as they are. And they're the same with you. You're easy to please.'

'Oh, thanks!'

'No, I don't mean it in a bad way. I mean – I mean, things make you happy really easily, you're laid back. You don't have to be the centre of attention in order to feel good.'

'But you're the centre of attention because you're so much fun.'

Autumn stops again and turns to me. 'Do I seem like much fun now?'

I don't reply.

'That's the problem, you see. I've spent my whole life being like that – but I can't do it any more, and now nothing works.'

'What doesn't work?'

'Me. My life,' she says. Her voice is dark and empty. 'I put on this act, make people think I'm coping, make them think I'm happy enough. I spent the first year after the accident looking after Mum and Dad, the second year falling apart myself, and the third – well, I don't even know where that's gone. It's as if I've disappeared altogether. I've turned into a paper thin image of who I really am – and you just showed that all up for the pretence it is.'

'How did I do that?'

Autumn smiles shyly. 'You reminded me what real friendship is.'

I can feel my cheeks burning. For a moment, it all feels worth it. Everything I've gone through over these last few days. It *is* all going to work out after all! Even if I end up trapped three years ahead forever, at least I'll have Autumn by my side. We'll be best friends for always. I'll tell her everything and we'll help each other cope with it all. She'll help me fill in the gaps, and I'll help her deal with everything that's happened to her. A huge weight feels like it's flying off me and into the distance.

And then Autumn speaks again, and the weight

boomerangs round and comes back to hit me flat in the stomach.

'But it's not enough,' she says.

'What? What isn't enough?'

'Any of it. It's too late.'

'I don't understand. Too late for what?'

Autumn shakes her head. 'For anything,' she says eventually. 'For everything.' Her voice comes out as a squeak, as though the words are being squeezed and strangled in her throat.

'Autumn, what are you talking about?' I repeat, taking a step closer towards her.

She wipes the back of her hand across her face. 'I can't – I can't . . . Please, just leave it, Jen.'

One look at her tear-stained face is all I need to let me know this is serious. 'No, I won't leave it,' I say firmly. A tiny part of me registers a split second of shock. I've *never* said no to Autumn before!

Autumn looks into my eyes. She takes a deep breath, and when she speaks, her voice is so soft it's like a whisper on a breeze. 'You remember last year, when I was so mean to you? I told you to stop living in a fantasy world? And I was so mad at Mum and Dad for hanging on to the smallest bits of hope?'

'I remember,' I say. It's not hard, seeing as it was only a few hours ago in my world.

'Well, I was wrong.'

'What d'you mean? You were wrong about what?'

'I thought that we'd all do better to face the truth. But I want the fantasy back,' she says.

I stop walking and turn to face her. 'Autumn, what are you trying to say?'

She stops as well, and looks at me. 'They've been seeing a counsellor for the last year. They've managed to drag me along a few times, too. He's helped them face the facts. Helped us all to come to terms with the reality. With what the doctors have been telling us all for three years. That all we're doing is prolonging the inevitable.'

There's a cold feeling that I can't explain slithering around inside my body. It creeps up my spine, snakes along the back of my neck, and comes to settle in my throat. 'I don't understand,' I say eventually. 'What are you trying to tell me?'

Autumn's shoulders shake as she drops her head. Her reply is barely audible. 'They wanted us to come here to make the decision – the place where it happened, the last place we were happy together. We talked last night, and we've all agreed. We tried to find a way round it, but we've spent so long clutching at straws, there's nothing left to get hold of.'

'Agreed what?' I ask, even though I'm pretty sure I know what she's about to say.

'We're telling the doctors when we get home: it's time to turn the machines off.' Autumn's eyes are green pools of tears. 'My little brother's going to die.' And with that, she falls against me and sobs so hard her whole body shakes. 'I can't bear it, Jenni. My baby brother. I'm going to lose him for ever.'

I wrap my arms round her as tight as I can, and try

to stop myself from crying with her. She needs me to be strong – and I'm going to be whatever she needs.

'Oh, Autumn. I wish I could change it,' I say as I hold her tight. 'I wish more than anything that I could.' Little Mikey. I saw him two days ago, right here. And now – it's unthinkable. It's impossible.

'I know,' she says. 'So do I. I've wished it every day for the last three years – wished we could have acted quicker at the time. Those three hours from when it happened to when he was finally scanned – how could a couple of measly hours make such a difference? Even one of them could have been enough to save him, enough to catch the bleed before it spread too far for them to operate. No one will ever know how much I've wished for those hours back – wished I'd never told him to gallop on that stupid horse, and wished I hadn't believed him when he said he felt fine after the fall.'

'Autumn, it's not your fault.'

'I know. I know. I'm past that. I know it's no one's fault. And I know that no one can change any of it. You can't turn back time and make it all different. I wish you could, though.'

That's when I realise. My arms suddenly feel heavy, and I let go of Autumn.

Can't you?

I've spent all this time thinking I'm trapped here for good – but there *has* to be a way to get back. There *has* to be. I know I can't go far enough back to stop it from happening, but if I could just get back to the present day, I could get back to a reality where Autumn still has three more years with her kid brother alive. Let her live those three years again. And now that I know what's ahead, I can be stronger for her; be a better friend; be by her side, no matter what. We could spend more time at the hospital, look after him better; maybe we could even do loads of research, find something out that could change all this – maybe even find a way of getting him out of the coma! Who says we couldn't?

I've *got* to be able to do something. I've got to at least *try* – or Mikey will be dead next week.

'Jenni, are you OK?' Autumn's staring at me.

'What?'

'Are you OK? You've gone pale.'

I pull my sleeve back to look at my watch. It's half one. In half an hour – three years ago – Autumn and her parents are going to get the news that Mikey's in a coma that the doctors believe to be permanent. I need to be with her when she hears this. We need to do the whole thing differently. I *have* to find a way.

'I've got to go,' I say suddenly.

'You're leaving me? Now? After everything I've just said?'

I take both of her hands in mine. 'Autumn, I'm not leaving you. I'm going to change it. Not everything, but some of it. I'm going to make it better.'

'But how – '

'I haven't got time,' I say, getting up again. 'Trust me, OK? Do you trust me?'

She nods.

'Right, I have to go, then.'

'Jenni,' she says softly.

I pause at her side. 'What?'

She swallows. 'I'm sorry. For everything. I'm sorry I pushed you away.'

I smile at my best friend. 'You've nothing to be sorry for,' I say. 'Nothing at all. It's going to be OK. You'll see.'

And then I run up the path, back to Autumn's block. Half an hour. I've got half an hour. I could make it. If I can just get back to the lift, if I can find a way of getting into it again somehow. There's *got* to be a way. I *can't* be stuck here forever.

I'm standing on the third floor, in front of the old lift. Correction, in front of where the old lift used to be. But there's absolutely no sign that it was ever there.

Maybe there never was another lift. Perhaps I really did lose my memory. Or imagined this entire thing. Maybe I really *am* losing my mind. I lean against the wall, letting my head fall against it. It makes a hollow thud.

Hollow. The wall's hollow. It's plasterboard! The lift must still be behind it! Maybe I can get to it after all. I hammer against it with my fists. But it's useless. All I'm doing is bruising my hands.

I search frantically around me. Nothing. The place is always so tidy, so perfect.

Then I remember the cupboard downstairs with all the logs in it. Maybe . . .

I tear down the stairs. The place where the old lift should be is exactly the same as the place on the third floor: sealed up, painted over, but hollow and flimsy. But it's not the lift I want; it's the door beside it. I throw the cupboard open. A couple of brushes are propped up along one side, a mop in a bucket along the other. I consider these for a second. Not heavy enough.

Then I spot it in the far corner. Bingo! The axe Mr Barraclough used for the logs!

I grab the axe and run back up to the third floor. I've got to come back to the ground floor in the lift. And I've got to hurry!

I'm panting by the time I get to the third floor. My chest feels as if it's got elastic bands wrapped tight around it. I run to the lift.

I've never done anything like this in my life. Jenni Green doesn't do things like this! Except, judging by today's events, it seems Jenni Green has changed. Autumn would be proud of me for what I'm about to do. Will I ever get to tell her? Would she believe me, even if I did?

I've no time to think about questions I can't answer. I've got to do this.

With a quick look around me to make sure there's no one there to see what I'm about to do – and a silent apology for what in anyone's book would amount to mindless vandalism – I lift the axe over my shoulder, take a deep breath, and smash it as hard as I can against the wall.

I've done it. There's a hole in the wall. Through it, I can see the metal door of the lift. It's still there, behind the wall, exactly as it was.

I just need to reach the button. I raise the axe again and again, cracking it against the wall until I've made a gap big enough to reach through. I feel around on the old wall behind the plasterboard. That's it. The button. I press it and wait.

Nothing happens.

I've made a hole big enough to climb through now, but there's nowhere to climb to. Just the old door standing closed in front of me. What am I going to do? This is my one and only chance to change this.

I press the button again. *Please, please, please work. I'll do anything. I'll be the best friend ever in the world, and the best daughter. I'll only ever think of others, never myself. I'll work hard at everything. Just please let me get into the lift!*

And then I hear it. The whirring noise. I leap up. It's happening. It's coming! My heart's banging so hard it's hurting my chest.

I clamber through the hole, open the first door wide enough to squeeze through, then pull the lift's inner door across. Without pausing to think, I close the doors behind me, slam my hand on to the button that says 'G' and hold my breath as the lift rattles into action.

The lift seems to creak downwards even more slowly and uncertainly than last time, shaking and juddering all the way. It sounds as if bits of metal are falling down the shaft below me. Eventually, it rattles to a halt and I pull the gate across, open the outer door and step out, glancing behind me to make sure the lift doesn't disappear the moment I've turned my back. It doesn't. It's still there.

I check my watch. Quarter to two.

Quarter to two? My heart drops so hard it's as if it's falling down a lift shaft itself. What was I *thinking*? I'm a complete and utter fool! There's no way I can get to the hospital in time. It takes at least twenty minutes to get there in the car. Half an hour if it's anyone except my dad driving.

That's when I realise, even if I could get to the hospital, what could I change anyway? I've been kidding myself – racing back to the past to try to stop something that's going to happen whether I'm there or not. I was so desperate to help, it didn't occur to me that the main thing I need to change is the accident – and there's *nothing* I can do to change that. It's already happened, and there are no buttons left to press in the lift. I can't go anywhere and I can't change anything.

The best I can hope for is that I can be a better friend this time around.

I tighten the belt on the jeans that are baggy again, get back in the lift and slump down against the wall, my head in my hands. Maybe I'll just sit here in a ball, hide in this lift and hope it'll all go away.

There's a noise in the foyer as someone comes in from outside. I jump up.

'Jenni!'

'Craig?' Six-year-old Craig! Cute, silly, messy-haired and gap-toothed Craig!

'*Thought* it was you!' he grins.

'What are you doing here?'

He nudges a thumb at the door. 'I saw you from outside. I've been talking to the workmen. Mum said I could, remember?'

I brush myself down and join him in the hallway. 'Come on, let's go back to the apartment.'

Outside, I take his hand and try to act normal. 'So what did the workmen tell you about this time?' I ask, ready to let him prattle away while my brain carries on being somewhere else.

'They told me all about what they're building over the road,' he says, his eyes shining with excitement. What is it about workmen that makes them so fascinating to six-year-old boys? 'They're making a new building where we can have table tennis and pool and table football,' he grins.

'Great. What else?'

'Um.' Craig presses a finger to his chin. 'That's it.' He swings my hand as we walk. 'Oh yes,' he says as we approach our block. 'They were telling me how that one – ' he points back at Autumn's block 'used to be a hotel, and all the posh people used to come there and the servants used to live in the basement and you never saw them and—'

I stop and pull him round to face me. 'The *what*?' My face has gone cold.

'The servants. You never saw them 'cos they—'

'Not the servants.' I pause while I catch my breath. 'The basement. You said there's a basement.'

'Yeah, that's where they lived.'

'Really?' I drop Craig's hand.

'What? What's wrong? What did I say?'

There's a basement! Maybe the lift could take me there. But it can't do – I've pressed all the buttons. There isn't one for any basement. But maybe I didn't look carefully enough. Maybe there is a way. 'I've got to do something.' I start walking briskly back to Autumn's block.

'I'm coming!' Craig runs after me.

'Go back to the apartment, Craig.'

'I'm coming with you.'

'No.'

'Where are you going?'

I quicken my pace. 'I don't know,' I say. It's true. I don't know where the lift will take me, or even if there *is* a basement. But it's got to be worth a try. It's my only hope – and I'm *not* giving up till I've tried everything.

'What are you doing?'

I ignore Craig as I scan the walls. *3, 2, 1, G.* That's it. I *have* been to every floor. My heart sinks heavily, dragging down my last shred of hope with it.

But wait. Maybe I *haven't* been to every floor. The piece of plywood underneath the buttons. Could it be hiding something?

I pull at it, but it's fixed hard.

'What are you doing?' Craig asks, craning his neck to watch as I pull hopelessly at the wood.

'Nothing. Leave me alone, Craig.'

He shrugs and wanders off – but a moment later he's back.

'Craig, I've told you to – '

'Here, use this,' he says. He's holding out a screw-driver.

I stare at him. 'How did you – where did you get that?'

'The workmen,' he says with the simple logic only possessed by six-year-old boys.

I grab the screwdriver, then I grab him as well and plant a big kiss on his cheek.

'Gerroff,' he says, wiping his cheek with his sleeve, but also looking secretly pleased with himself.

I work at the old screws, and eventually, I've undone them all. The plywood falls away – and I gasp as I see what's underneath. A cracked, wobbly button – and next to it, the letter *B*.

The basement! There really *is* a basement!

Where will it take me? A year back? I try to remember

what my life was like a year ago. Can I face going through the whole year again?

I don't even have to think about it. Mikey will be dead next week. I don't have a choice. This is it. My one chance to change all this – to *really* change it.

'Craig, go back to the apartment,' I say, shoving him out of the lift.

'I'm staying with you!'

'You're not. Go home.'

'No!' he pouts.

I take a tight breath. 'OK. But you can't come in with me. Wait here.'

Before he can argue, I pull the doors closed and stare at the button till my eyes water and the letter blurs. I've got to do it.

The button wobbles and sticks as I touch it. Pressing it hard, I watch as Craig's face disappears from the little window and the lift clunks and squeaks and whirrs, taking me down to the basement.

13

itch black.

I can't see a thing. I step carefully out of the lift and crash straight into a box on the floor. As I stop to rub my toe, my eyes gradually adjust to the dark. I can make out a few vague shapes: boxes and planks of wood and overflowing bin bags everywhere. A giant junk room. I stumble to the opposite wall and feel around for a light, praying there aren't any rats.

Found it. A switch high up on the wall. I flick it and the room bounces into view as a strip light flashes on. There's a steel door in the far corner. The only way out, it looks like. I head towards it, making sure not to trip over anything.

Please, please don't be locked.

It is.

No! One steel door, locked solid. I push and pull at the handle. The door doesn't move a centimetre.

I scramble round the room, lifting boxes, heaving trunks around, looking for something, anything that could get me out of here. I scan the ceiling. There's a fancy panel all round the top edges of the walls. An air vent, maybe? There's a tiny grill in one corner, too high for me to reach, even if I stood on a box – and about as big as my hand.

I slump down on to a box. There *must* be something; there has to be. I scan every bit of the room. Nothing. Not even a window.

'Craig!' My voice echoes round the room, fading back to silence.

What am I doing calling Craig? Even if I hadn't gone back in time, he'd be a whole floor above me. And if I've got my calculations right, he won't be there for another year!

I can't believe it. No way out. Well, there's *one* way out – back to the present. The lift is standing open, waiting for me.

All this, and I've failed?

Wait! No. I'm *not* going to let that happen. Maybe the old Jenni would have given up, but this one doesn't.

I'll think of something. Perhaps I can go back up and get Mr Barraclough's axe, get through the outside door. Or get enough food and water to last a couple of days – long enough for someone to come down to the basement and let me out. Or perhaps I'll think of an even better idea. I'll do something – anything! As long as I can figure out how to get out of this building from the basement, I'll have a whole year before the accident happens. I can stop it – I can!

My heart leaping so hard it feels as if it's about to

jump out of my mouth, I close myself back inside the lift, and press G.

I'm going to do this. I'm going to change things.

I hold my breath as the lift trundles upwards, getting slower and slower, the rattling and creaking growing louder and louder, the scraping noises spreading out into a slow screech. *Come on, come on. Get me back to the ground floor!*

More creaking, clanking, clattering.

And then it stops.

I pull the doors across – to be faced with a grey brick wall!

The lift has got stuck just below the ground floor! Above the wall, I can see the floor of the foyer. If I jump up, I could probably get back up there.

'Craig!' I call out again. Where is he? Why didn't he wait for me? *'Craig!'* I shout louder. Nothing.

I grip on to the ledge in front of me, scrabbling up the wall and heaving myself over the top and out of the lift. I clamber out, pulling myself up on my stomach. My jeans are covered in dust; so's my hair, but it doesn't matter. At least I'm out. I'm back at the ground floor.

I get up quickly, just as a young couple pass me. They're smiling, their hands entwined. They look familiar. Have I seen them before?

I dust myself off in front of the ornate mirror. For a moment, it looks strange to see me as twelve-year-old Jenni once more. My clothes are loose again. My hair's back to how it was, hanging loose in long, ring-letty curls.

I shake myself away from my reflection and focus my thoughts. I just need to stay calm. I can figure this out. I *can* change this; I've got plenty of time.

I'll go back to the apartment and make a plan. I just need to think of something before we leave here.

I've got till the end of the week to figure this out.

The telly's blaring as I open the door into the apartment.

'Craig, how many times do I have to tell you? Turn it OFF!' Dad's voice blares over it.

'Where did you get to?' I ask Craig. He's sitting cross-legged on the living room floor, fixing a car while he watches the television.

'What?' He looks up, confused.

Dad comes out of the kitchen. 'Forget something?' he calls.

'Huh?'

He dries his hands and wanders back into the living room. 'You'll miss them if you don't get a move on,' he says.

'Miss who?'

Dad laughs. 'Who d'you think? Don't you *want* to go horse riding?'

My mouth freezes as a chill creeps round my face and neck. 'Horse riding?' I ask slowly.

'You all right, love?' Dad says, looking at me with concern as Mum comes into the room. Big, round, eight months pregnant Mum. 'You've gone white.'

'Mum,' I gasp, turning round. Then I look back at Dad. 'What day is it?' I ask, my voice hoarse.

'Sunday, all day,' Dad says. 'At least it was last time I looked.' He holds an arm out towards Mum. She smiles at him and strokes his arm.

It's happened! I've gone back in time. The lift – it never made it back to the ground floor. That must be it. I've gone back a day! One day. I look at my watch. It's ten to two. On Sunday! I've still got time!

'I have to go,' I gasp.

'Crikey, where's the fire?' Dad says. 'Hold your horses.' He turns to Mum. 'See what I did there? Hold your horses. Might have to write that down.'

Mum smiles indulgently at him.

I run to the door. 'Mum,' I say, turning round before I go.

She looks up.

I take a breath. How am I going to put this so she'll take notice of me? 'You have to take it easy today,' I say. 'Please, look after yourself. Don't rush, don't get stressed.'

Mum laughs. 'Stressed? I'm on holiday!'

'Really,' I insist. 'I mean it. Just go carefully, all right? I don't want you to go to the candle museum. Please. It's too much for you.'

'A candle museum is too much for me? Jen, I'm only pregnant, I'm not—'

'Please, Mum. You're not *only* pregnant. You're eight months pregnant, and you need to relax. Please.'

Mum meets my eyes as though she's looking at someone she doesn't recognise. Well, she wouldn't do. She's never had a daughter who's put her foot down and told people what to do before!

'OK, ' she says eventually. 'You're right. I've actually been feeling a bit more tired than I've been letting on. Maybe I do need to take it easy. Craig will be fine playing here.'

'Good. And, Dad, you need to cancel your squash match.'

Dad looks shocked. 'Cancel my—'

'Dad! It's important. Come on, we all know you're no good at squash anyway,' I say with a big smile so he knows I'm not intentionally being mean. I need him to listen to me. 'Dad, you have to stay and look after Mum – and you need to pick us up from horse riding. Please.'

Dad looks at Mum. 'D'you know what? I think you're probably right,' he says, stroking Mum's stomach. 'I don't think a game of squash is the most important thing in my life at the moment. I'll phone Mr Andrews now and tell him.'

I let out a breath as I try to figure out if there's anything else. I have to be prepared, cover all bases. 'And Dad – be early, OK?'

'Why?'

I cross my fingers behind my back, hoping no one will know I'm lying. 'Just that Autumn said they usually finish the rides early and we don't want to be waiting around too long.'

'Oh, the glamorous life of a taxi driver,' Dad says dramatically.

I give him a kiss on the cheek. 'Thanks, Dad.' With any luck, I won't even need Dad to come at all, but at least I know he'll be there – just in case.

I whizz upstairs to get my horse riding gear. When I come down, Dad's just putting the phone down. 'Cancelled squash,' he says. 'See you later.'

'Thanks, Dad. See you in a bit.' I give them both a hug, praying that the next time I seem them won't be in the middle of any kind of disaster, and hoping neither of them has noticed I'm shaking.

Then I have one last thought. 'Oh, and Dad,' I say, forcing my voice to sound as casual as possible. 'On your way, go and have a look at Mile End Farm, will you?'

'Mile End Farm – what's that?'

It's where the accident took place – not that I could tell him that.

'Look it up,' I say. 'Ask someone – it's just somewhere I've heard about and thought we might like to visit. Thought you could check it out and pick up some leaflets on the way. Please just do it.'

I feel slightly bad about lying to Dad. But it's the best thing I can think of. And if he figures out that it's actually someone's private address and not a place to have a family day out after all, I'll just tell him I made a mistake. The important thing is to make sure he's there if we need him.

Dad shrugs and gives Mum a puzzled look. 'Whatever you say,' he replies.

I smile at him. 'Thanks, Dad,' I say.

And then I turn and run.

Please let me get there on time. Please!

I've got five minutes. Two o' clock on the dot, she said. Please don't let my watch be slow.

I'm breathless as I reach her block. The car's there. The Porsche. They've not left! I've never been so pleased to see a flashy red sports car in my life!

I hesitate for the briefest of moments by the lift. I daren't do it. Not even the normal one.

I run along the corridor and up the stairs, my throat on fire. Pausing outside the door, a flicker of fear rushes through me. What if they're not here? What if it's Mrs Smith again? What if it wasn't the lift at all but something else, and Autumn's still—

'Jenni!' Autumn's standing in the door, grinning widely. 'You just made it. Come on, Mum's taking us.' She pulls me through the door.

'Where's Mikey?' I ask. I have to see him for myself.

And then he wanders out of his bedroom, electronic game in his hand, mouth pursed in concentration. I run over to him, kneel down and hug him tightly.

'Eurgh! Geddof!' he says.

I laugh. 'He's OK!' I say. I can't help myself.

Autumn tips her head to the side and rolls her eyes in my direction, as if I've lost the plot. 'Err, I think so,' she says. Then she goes over and feels Mikey's forehead, and tickles him under his chin till he giggles and pushes her away. 'Yep. He's as OK as he'll ever be, anyway.'

Mrs Leonard comes into the hallway. 'Right, are we ready?' she asks.

'Just finishing this game,' Mikey says.

'You can play it later,' Mrs Leonard tells him. 'Come on, we'll be late.'

I stare at Mikey, then Autumn, then their Mum. 'Mikey's not coming,' I say. 'It's just me and Autumn.'

'Dad just got a call from Mr Andrews,' Autumn says. 'Apparently he's got a squash court booked and someone's cancelled on him at the last minute, so Dad's going to play. Mikey'll have to tag along with us. Mum's going to see if he can come out on the hack with us. He's ridden before so there shouldn't be a problem.'

I stare at Autumn. My insides have turned to ice. 'You're kidding me.' I don't believe it. I've managed to get back here, stop Mum from going out *and* get Dad to pick us up – and in the process I've made sure that Mikey goes riding!

Maybe fate has decided what's going to happen to Mikey and there's absolutely nothing I can do to stop it. Maybe that's how it works: I could go back in time a hundred times – and still achieve nothing. The same thing would happen to Mikey every time.

I think I'm going to be sick.

Autumn pulls a face. 'It's a pain, isn't it?'

I can't even reply.

Mrs Leonard's on her way down the drive. 'Come on kids, we're going to be late. Mikey, leave your game.'

I grab Autumn's arm. I'm not ready to give up and let fate take over just yet. 'Autumn, Mikey can't come with us!'

'I know. It's so unfair, but there's nothing we can do. He can't stay here on his own.'

'He could go over to my house, hang out with Craig.'

'I don't want to hang out with Craig. I want to go horse riding,' Mikey says, shoving past us and running to the car. 'I'm having the front seat!'

I clench my fingers into fists by my side. 'Autumn, he can't come,' I hiss. 'We can't let him.'

Autumn laughs. 'Hey, don't get too worked up about it. It'll be fine; we don't need to talk to him.'

'It's not that,' I say, squeezing into the back of the car with Autumn squashed in next to me.

She looks at me. 'What is it?' she asks, an edge of defensiveness creeping into her voice. 'We do enough things with your family; why's it such a problem to have my kid brother come with us?'

'I – I can't explain. It just is,' I say, scratching around for another idea. If I can't persuade her to stop Mikey from coming with us, I'll have to somehow pull the plug on the whole trip.

'Look, it's me, OK? I don't want to go. I want to do something else,' I say. I lean forward, as well as I can manage in the tiny space, and tap Mrs Leonard's shoulder. 'Um, actually, I've changed my mind about going horse riding.'

Autumn bursts out laughing. 'You're messing about, aren't you?'

Mrs Leonard glances at me in the rear view mirror. 'Are you OK, Jenni?'

'No, not really. I feel a bit – um, sick. I don't think I can go riding. Can we do something different?' Then I remember today's trip. 'Can we go to the candle museum instead?'

Autumn guffaws and punches me on the arm. 'You're hilarious!' she says. 'I love it.'

Mrs Leonard smiles indulgently at us both. 'You two,' she says. 'Right, seatbelts on – we need to get there.'

And then she drives Autumn, Mikey and me to the stables, and I can't speak another word all the way there. All I can think is: I can't let this happen. After everything I've lived through in the last couple of days, I can't have made it back here only to let the whole thing happen all over again. Only this time, it's going to happen in front of my eyes.

I'll have to think of something else. I've still got time. Maybe I can talk to someone at the stables. Get them to call off the hack, say the horses are all sick, they haven't got enough staff, it's too hot to go out – anything! There's only one thing I know: I've got to stop Mikey from getting on that horse.

Autumn gets out of the car and marches ahead with Mikey. I trail behind with Mrs Leonard.

'Can't Mikey stay with you?' I say uselessly.

'I've got a beauty treatment, love, and then I'm meeting my husband for a date at the aromatherapy room after his squash match,' she says, laughing. 'Hey, what's wrong with Mikey all of a sudden? You've never minded him being around before.'

We cross a dusty yard and head towards the far corner. A wooden 'reception' sign is nailed on to the wall.

Inside, a bunch of excited girls are queuing up with their parents. A woman behind a small desk is scribbling something on a form. She gets up to fetch a couple of hats. Bits of straw litter the ground; a leathery smell wafts across the room.

Mikey runs over. 'She says I can go, too,' he says, grinning as the woman comes over to him with a hat in her hand.

'Try this one,' she says, handing Mikey the hat. She looks familiar. Where have I seen her before?

As she turns to us and smiles, I realise where I've seen her. It's the woman from the news programme!

My body judders. It's going to happen. Soon – within hours – and no one knows it except me. It's still going to happen!

Everyone's acting so normal: smiling, laughing, trying on hats. How can they do that? I can't just stand back and watch it happen, I can't!

Autumn takes the hat she's offered and goes to wait

outside in the yard. I follow her when I've got mine sorted and we say goodbye to her mum.

'Autumn, please listen,' I say, my voice low so no one else can hear me. I'm going to tell her the truth. I've no choice.

'Come on, Jen. Just go with it,' she says, grinning as she fastens the strap on her hat. 'You never know, it might even be as much fun as the candle museum.' Then she bursts out laughing.

I take a breath. 'It's not safe. Something awful is going to happen to Mikey if he comes horse riding today.'

She stops what she's doing. 'Oh, Jenni. Please don't do this.'

'Do what?'

'Resort to sci-fi stories as a way to get me to listen. If you don't want to come, don't, but *please* stop trying to spoil it for me and my brother. Give him a break.'

'Autumn, just *listen* to me!' I snap, 'I'm not trying to spoil it for you *or* Mikey. I'm trying to warn you!'

'Warn me? So you can see into the future now, can you? What are you, Mystic Meg?'

The woman from the stables has come out of the office. 'Right, all those on the hack, this way,' she says, striding off to a row of stables on the other side of the yard. Autumn hurries after her. 'I'm Carol, by the way,' the woman calls over her shoulder as she walks. There are nine of us. Four girls who look about my age, all giggling together; a gangly boy on his own, pacing awkwardly along behind them; an older couple, and the three of us.

How am I going to stop this from happening?

I scurry to the front of the group, following just behind Carol and Autumn. Carol stops at the first stable. 'This is Hunter,' she says, stroking his nose. 'Very good natured, easy to control, but powerful when he wants to be. Mark, you can take him; you've ridden him before, haven't you?'

The gangly boy blushes and nods quickly.

Moving on, Carol casts her eye over the group. 'Marion,' she says, motioning the older woman to come forward. 'You want to take Star?'

'Okey doke,' Marion smiles, tickling the horse's nose.

Carol moves on to the next stable. 'Now, here's one of our new boys,' she says, reaching in to pat the horse in the next stable. The horse jerks its head up, batting her hand away. It's got a dark brown nose, a thin white stripe running down the centre. 'He's only young, and he's a darling. He'll be suitable for one of the children. He can be a bit of a feisty little fellow this one,' she smiles, 'but nice as pie if you keep him in check.'

Mikey steps forward. 'He's lovely,' he says. 'What's his name?'

'Angus.'

My blood runs cold. *Angus*. Mikey takes another step forward, reaching out to stroke him.

'I'm having him!' I burst out. It's him! The horse from the telly. The one that threw Mikey off.

'You?' Autumn snorts. 'I thought you didn't even want—'

'I'm having him,' I repeat.

Carol turns to me. 'Can you ride?' she asks.

'Yes,' I say firmly. Autumn opens her mouth to speak. 'I've ridden loads,' I add quickly. 'Please let me ride Angus.'

Carol looks me up and down. 'OK,' she smiles. 'You're about the right height.'

She moves on, the rest of the group following her to the next stable. 'Now, this is Mouse,' I hear her say. She points to Mikey. 'Same size as Angus. Not quite so spirited but keen as mustard on the open country. Want to take him?'

Mikey agrees. Autumn takes the next horse along. She's called Winter. As the group moves on, she gives her horse a stroke before turning to look at me over her shoulder. 'What are you playing at?' she asks.

'I'm not playing at anything.'

'Yes you are. Pretending to be Mrs Keen when you don't even want to be here. What's going on?'

'I just liked the look of Angus. Anything wrong with that?'

I glance across at Mikey. He's still stroking his horse. Mouse nuzzles into Mikey's shoulder as Autumn shrugs and turns away.

'Come on, Jenni,' Carol calls from her horse. Everyone else has got on and is waiting for me, surrounding me in the yard.

I try to smile as I stand next to Angus, gripping the bridle and praying he won't stand on my foot. Carol jumps down from her horse. 'Come on,' she says. 'I'll give you a leg up.'

She reaches up to Autumn and hands her the reins to her horse. 'You look confident enough up there. Hold on to Misty for a minute, would you?'

Autumn watches me as she takes the reins.

'Bend your leg,' Carol says, standing behind me and heaving me up into the air. Oh heck, she's lifting me on to the horse!

I'm up. High up in the air, clutching the reins. 'Thanks,' I say, my voice shaking.

'Adjust your stirrups,' Carol says.

I look down at my feet. *Adjust my stirrups? How do I do that?*

With a sigh, Carol comes back to my side. 'Bend your leg forward,' she says, then yanks at a strap under the saddle. She walks round to the other side and does the same.

'You sure you've ridden before?' she asks.

'Yeah, loads,' I say, forcing a laugh. 'I just didn't hear you properly.'

'OK, well ride at the back with me to begin with, so I can keep an eye on you. He can get a bit frisky, Angus can. Just keep a firm grip on the reins, OK?'

'OK,' I say woodenly. And then she's moving away and jumping back on to her horse.

'Walk on, everybody,' she calls, waving the riders past her. She indicates a girl on horseback ahead of us who must work at the stables too. 'Sue will lead from the front. I'll stay at the back. The rest of you, stay in between us, OK?'

'You crazy lady,' Autumn says with a laugh as she passes me. 'Least we're here though. It's not all that bad, is it?'

'No, it's great,' I say through gritted teeth.

Autumn laughs again before kicking her horse and trotting on to catch up with Mikey, who's up ahead walking alongside Mark.

I copy everyone's movements, squeezing my legs into the horse's sides. 'Come on, Angus,' I say under my breath. 'Be good for me.' He pulls at the reins, stretching his head out and making me lurch forwards in my seat before he settles into a steady walk.

The hack takes us down into a disused railway track that's been turned into a walkway. Trees reach across the top, in a ferny arch. Flies buzz around the horses' heads as we walk along in a line, hooves thudding gently on the ground.

Angus is behaving himself perfectly. I'm even starting to enjoy it. It's easy. All I have to do is hold on to the reins and sit still. He does the rest.

'We're turning here,' Sue calls from up at the front. I look to see where she's pointing. The track leads up through the trees to another path higher up.

'There are some lovely open fields up here where we can have a bit of a canter.'

'Excellent,' one of the girls in front of me says to the girl alongside her. 'I thought we were going to be stuck down here all afternoon.'

'Boring!' her friend replies.

The horses turn up towards the high path. 'Come on, Angus,' I whisper. 'Up here.' He stops at the bottom of the new path. 'Come *on*,' I repeat. Nothing. He won't move.

Carol's right behind me. 'Give him a kick,' she says. 'Walk on, Angus,'

I bounce my heels against his sides like I've seen the others do. Angus pulls on the bridle, yanking me forwards.

'Steady,' Carol says. She rides round to my side and tugs gently on the bridle. Angus jerks his head up again but still doesn't move. I grip the reins with sweaty palms. *Come on Angus, please don't do this.*

Carol gives him a tap with her whip. He gives one more yank on the reins, rearing up slightly before settling down again. 'Give him another squeeze,' she says again. 'Just gently. Use your knees.'

I squeeze my knees into his sides and he finally edges forward. As he follows the others up the path, I breathe a sigh of relief. My heart's racing.

The path takes us up to a wide meadow. I can't see the end of it. All I can see is green open fields. Is this where Autumn encouraged Mikey to gallop? A thought crashes into my head so hard it takes my breath away:

what if it happens to me? What if Angus gallops across the field and I'm the one who's thrown off, I'm the one who ends up –

'OK, gather round me, everyone,' Carol calls the group together, thankfully breaking into my thoughts. 'Those of you who are happy to have a canter here can do so. We're heading over there to the stream and the woods.' She points to some trees in the distance. 'Hands up who's ready to do that?'

The group of girls raise their hands. So does Autumn. The only people who don't are Mark, Mikey, me and the older couple.

'Mikey, you can canter – come with us,' Autumn whispers.

'He's fine with me!' I snap, before he can reply. Autumn just gives me a funny look and goes off with the other girls.

'Right, you go ahead with Sue,' Carol says. 'The rest of you stay close to me, OK?'

I nod, holding tightly on to the reins as I watch the others charge across the field, Autumn racing ahead at the front. Mikey's just ahead of me. Safe. I'm starting to breathe almost normally again. *Nearly there, nearly there.*

'We'll just take it at a steady trot,' Carol says. 'You guys OK with that?'

As we set off, I bounce around in the saddle, jigging and slipping. I hang around behind the others so they won't notice. Every time Carol looks round, I try to lift myself in the stirrups like the others are doing.

'Just along that river for a bit, then down a lane to Mile End Farm and that's our halfway point,' Carol calls to us.

Mile End Farm! My throat tightens another notch.

'Sounds fine,' I force myself to say. The others smile and nod.

As we approach the river, I recognise the surroundings. It's where they filmed the news report. We're near the farm now. *This is where it happened.*

They're all waiting on the other side of the river. Even Mikey's already gone across.

But I can't do it. The horse, Angus, he galloped up to the river, and plunged down the bank without slowing. That's how Mikey was thrown off. And now he's going to do it to me. It's all going to happen to me instead!

No. No, it doesn't have to be like that. I'm not galloping, I'm not Mikey, I've changed the past. I'm safe. I can do it.

'Come on, Jenni.' Carol's calling from behind me I'm gripping the reins tight, yanking Angus's head upright and making him dance jerkily at the water's edge. If I'm not careful, I'll make him buck me off. I've got to cross it.

Autumn's watching me from the other side, laughter in her eyes. Mikey is next to her, staring at me like all the others.

'Come on Jenni. What're you waiting for?' he calls.

Why don't any of you understand? This is serious!

Then Angus makes his own mind up and walks into the water. I can't look. I've virtually got my eyes closed as he gracefully steps across. Two seconds later, we've

226

done it. We're across! I want to scream and laugh. We've avoided the accident! I've changed everything! It's not happened to Mikey and it's not going to happen to me either!

I'm so desperate to tell someone. I wish Autumn would listen to me. All the things we've talked about, all the sci-fi stories we've shared, maybe she really *would* understand, if I could think of the right way to tell her. I'll find a way, one day.

As we head up the lane, I can feel my confidence growing. I pass a couple of the girls, making my way towards Autumn at the front. I'll tell her everything, I'll make it into a joke or something. I'll enjoy the second hour of the hack as we head back to the stables. It's all going to be OK; I know it is. Mikey's riding alongside Autumn, the two of them confident and happy – I feel almost as confident as they look now I've stopped the accident.

'Autumn!' I call her as I pass the rest of the group. I'm grinning, waiting for her to turn as I go round the outside of the two girls behind her.

'Jenni, get in!' Carol shouts from behind me. 'You're in the middle of the road!'

It all happens so quickly.

The car comes from behind me. Too fast. Tearing along a little country lane at about 80 miles an hour, zooming past, virtually scraping into me.

Angus jumps up, throwing his head high. I grip the reins. Mikey turns at that moment, to see what's happening. I can see the horror in his eyes.

Pulling hard on the reins, somehow I manage to get Angus to the side of the road. I'm panting, almost breathless with fear and relief. That was *so* close.

But then I look up. I almost see it happen in slow motion, frame by frame. Mikey's horse, unsettled by the car, veers out into the road and rears up like a rodeo horse as the car disappears into the distance. Mikey's face is sheer terror. He's slipping in the saddle, grasping the horse's mane, his body hurled forwards again as Mouse plunges back to the ground.

'Autumn! Help!' he yells. Mouse is kicking out with his back legs now. Mikey's completely lost control.

Mikey. My throat closes up.

And then he's in the air. Mouse has thrown him off. One silent, almost calm, moment. And then the worst sound in the world – a sickening thud as Mikey meets the ground.

People are leaping off their horses. I just sit, staring open-mouthed at my best friend's little brother lying motionless on the road.

It's just like before. I can't speak, can't utter a word.

All this. Everything I've been through, and it didn't change a thing.

14

I jump down from Angus and pass the reins to Mark, who's pulled up alongside me. Everyone's getting off their horses and crowding round Mikey. I join Autumn by his side.

'Mikey, can you hear me?' I ask breathlessly.

Then Mikey opens his eyes and frowns at me. 'Course I can,' he says. And then he slowly sits up. He sits up! He's all right!

Rubbing his head, he carefully gets to his feet.

'Mikey, are you sure you're all right?' Autumn asks, holding on to his arm.

He shakes her off. 'I'm fine, sis. No big deal.'

A moment later, Carol's in front of him. 'Mikey? Where does it hurt?' she asks.

'It's just my head. Just banged it a bit. I'm fine, honestly!'

I'm so relieved I can't speak. I changed it – I really changed it. Mikey's fine. Everything's going to be OK!

And then something happens that feels sickeningly

familiar, but I can't think why. Carol takes her horse back from Sue and walks Mikey's horse over to her. 'Take Mouse back will you?' she says. 'I think Mikey should ride back with me on Magic.'

'I'm OK. Stop fussing everyone,' Mikey says. 'I can ride back.'

Carol shakes her head. 'Just to be on the safe side.' Then she helps him up on to her horse, and gets on behind him. 'We'll take it nice and slowly back to the stables. Follow me, guys. Sue, you bring up the rear this time.'

She starts to walk away, Mikey sitting in front of her, all the others starting to follow after them. And I can't move. I can't speak. I can't do anything – because I've realised something terrible. Something I only know from the news report that will be on television tonight.

This is exactly what happened last time.

'Come on, slowcoach, what you waiting for?' Autumn says, as she pulls up alongside me on her horse. We're walking up the lane alongside Mile End Farm. I'm trying to figure out what I can say to Carol, and what I can do to change this – even though part of me can't help wondering whether Mikey really *is* all right. He certainly seems it.

'That was close, wasn't it? Thought he was a gonner for a minute there!' Autumn says with a laugh.

How can she laugh?

I'm trying to figure out how to reply, when a car turns into the lane ahead of us.

Dad! He's here!

He pulls up and gets out of his car, just as Carol and Mikey reach him. They stop beside the car. I kick Angus on, to catch up with them.

'Hey, what's happened here then? Got lazy did you?' Dad asks Mikey with a wink.

Mikey grimaces at Dad. 'I'm fine,' he says. 'Fell off my horse, so they won't let me go back on my own. But I'm OK, honestly. Just bumped my head a bit.'

As I pull up alongside Carol and Mikey, Dad glances across at me and smiles. 'Hey sweetheart, you having a good time?'

A good time? Am I having a good time? I look across at Mikey. That's when I notice the back of his head. It's swollen up like a tennis ball. Suddenly I can see that things aren't quite how they seem. What was it Autumn said earlier? The surgeon's words: that the bleed had spread too far for them to operate because he hadn't been brought to hospital in time. That even one hour could have made all the difference. How Autumn wished she hadn't believed Mikey when he said he was fine.

With a shiver that shoots through me so hard it makes my whole body shake, I realise I haven't changed anything – yet. But perhaps there's still time.

'Dad, you need to take Mikey to hospital,' I say, my voice croaky and cracked with fear.

Mikey lets out a breath. 'Please, can everyone stop fussing. I'm *fine!*'

'We'll get him back to the stables and see how he is then,' Carol says. 'He's safe here with me. We'll be back there in an hour.'

An hour till we're back to the stables? That's too long! What can I do? I have to make them listen!

'Dad! Please. He needs to get to hospital now!' I say. This time, the fear has turned to panic. It's searing through my throat like fire. 'Don't listen to Mikey. He's worse than he thinks. If we take him to the stables, it'll be too late!'

Dad gives me a really strange look. As though he doesn't understand me, or doesn't recognise me or something. Well, he wouldn't. Here I am again, Jenni Green, the quiet one who doesn't make a fuss, barking orders at everyone.

'*Please*, Dad,' I say. 'I don't often ask things of you – but I'm asking this. Please listen to me. We need to get him to hospital. Now!'

Dad looks at me. Then across at Mikey. Then he nods. 'OK, hold on,' he says to me. 'Wait up a minute,' he calls to Carol.

Carol turns round in her saddle.

'Can I just have a quick word with Mikey?' he asks. Before Carol can answer, he adds, 'I'm a first aider.'

She turns the horse round to face Dad and he smiles up at Mikey. 'OK, little fellah, let's have a look at your head.' Mikey turns his head round so Dad can see. There's a lump the size of a golf ball. I clap a hand over

232

my mouth to stop me gasping out loud. I don't want to scare Mikey. Dad lets out a sharp breath. 'That's quite a lump you've got there, kid,' he says.

Mikey doesn't say anything.

'Mikey, do you feel sick at all?'

'No, I've told you. I'm OK.'

'Have you had a nosebleed?'

'Nope.'

'Does your neck hurt?'

Mikey doesn't reply.

'Mikey, is your neck sore?'

Mikey nods. 'Yes. Why? What does that mean? I just pulled it when I fell.'

'I'm sure you did,' Dad says calmly. 'I'm just checking. OK, can you tell me where you are, Mikey?'

Mikey laughs. 'On a horse,' he says sarcastically.

'And where are you on holiday?' Dad persists.

Mikey stares at Dad. Dad stares at Mikey. All of us stare at them both. Mikey's face has turned red. 'I'm at ... I'm at ... I can't remember what it's called,' he says eventually.

Dad holds two fingers in the air. 'How many fingers am I holding up?'

Mikey squints at Dad's hand. 'Um . . . I can't . . . Wait a minute, hold them properly. You're moving them about.'

Dad's hand is completely still.

'Can you tell me how many fingers, Mikey?'

Mikey stares at Dad's hand, his face gritted in concentration. 'Three? Four?' he says eventually.

Dad walks right up to the horse and reaches out for Mikey. 'That's it,' he says. 'I'm taking him to hospital.'

Suddenly, everything changes. Dad's lifting Mikey off the horse. Carol's jumped down too; the atmosphere feels as though someone has shot a bolt of electricity through it.

'Autumn, Jenni, let's go. Can someone take your horses?'

Carol grabs Angus's reins as I jump down. Sue rides over to Autumn to take her horse. 'We'll sort it,' she says.

A moment later, we're getting in the car. Mikey's in between Autumn and me, and Dad's starting the engine.

Mikey's turned pale. He doesn't look quite so fine any more. He looks more like a scared little boy.

Autumn squeezes his hand. 'Hey, don't worry bro,' she says. 'You'll be fine. Everything will be fine. We're just getting you checked out.'

I want to say something helpful, but I can't find the words. All I can think is: *will he?* Will any of this be fine? Will we get him to a doctor in time to prevent the future I've already seen? The future where Mikey never *ever* recovers from this? Or are we all fated to go through exactly the same thing, no matter how many times I try to come back and change it?

Dad catches my eye in the mirror. There's a question on his face. *How did you know?* he's asking. *What made you think I'd need to be here?*

I haven't got an answer – not one that he'd believe anyway – so I look away before he asks it out loud and

I'm forced to think of something. I turn to Autumn. 'It'll be OK,' I say. 'Whatever happens to Mikey. I'll never desert you. I'll be by your side; I'll do anything you need – you're never going to lose me. You need to remember that. We'll always be best friends, OK?'

Autumn gives me a puzzled look. 'I know that,' she says simply, with an attempt at a smile. And then I go back to staring out of the window, with only one thought: *Please let him be all right.* I say it over and over in my head, biting my nails so far down my skin is sore.

Please, please let him be all right.

I'm sitting on a plastic chair in a hospital waiting room, holding Autumn's hand. Mum's on the other side of me, her mum on the other side of her. Our dads are walking up and down in the corridor. Craig's sitting on the floor, playing with his cars.

Mikey's in a room with some doctors, having his head scanned.

No one is saying anything. It's as if all the sound has been sucked out of the world, along with all the colour, and the joy. All that is left is this waiting. And the question going round and round in my head: *did we get him here in time?*

'Tom.' Mum breaks the silence. Dad and Mr Leonard both turn to look at her. She points down the corridor. 'The doctor's coming back.'

At last.

Dad and Mr Leonard rush back to join us and the doctor comes over and pulls another chair across for himself. He's sitting down; that's not good, is it?

'Are you all family?' he asks.

Mum opens her mouth to speak but Mr Leonard beats her to it. 'Yes,' he says firmly. 'Doctor Wilson, just tell us how Mikey is.' He reaches out to take Mrs Leonard's hand. 'Please.'

The doctor breathes in. 'Mikey's had a nasty knock on his head,' he says. 'The CT scan shows that he's had something called an extra-dural haematoma. That's a bleed inside his head.'

Mrs Leonard makes a strange choking sound. Mum claps a hand over her mouth. I shut my eyes. I don't know how I think this'll help. If I could shut my ears, I'd do that too. Anything to put off what he's about to say.

The doctor is still talking. 'He's being treated as we speak,' he says. 'As soon as we've operated, we'll be able to tell you the situation more accurately. But I *can* tell you that, barring any unforeseen circumstances, he will almost certainly make a full recovery.'

'A *what*?' I yelp. Did he just say what I thought he said? He can't have. I must have heard wrong. I need to be sure. 'Can you say that again?'

The doctor turns to me and smiles. As he does so, I can't help wondering if this is the very same doctor who saw Autumn and her family in the other version of this moment. Were they sitting on these very chairs?

Did he smile at them that time too?

'All our investigations tell us that Mikey's going to be fine,' he says. 'He'll have a bit of a sore head for a week or so, and a great story for his friends – but that's about it. If you hadn't got him here so quickly, this could have been very different. Another hour and the bleed could well have developed to a point beyond our control.'

'What would that have meant?' Autumn asks.

Dr Wilson shakes his head. 'It's hard to say for sure. But, potentially, brain damage, coma … it could have even been fatal.' He turns to Dad. 'But thanks to you, Mr Green, I'm sure young Mikey is going to be just fine.'

I look over at Dad. He's staring at me. His eyes are watery. I've never seen my dad cry. Ever. He tries to speak. Then he scratches his forehead and shakes his head. 'It was Jenni,' he croaks, eventually. 'It was all thanks to Jenni.'

Dr Wilson comes over to me and looks right into my eyes. 'Well you, my dear, are a brave, smart and lucky young lady. You don't even want to *think* about what this could have meant without your actions.'

'No,' I reply, banishing the pictures in my head of the world where I know *exactly* what it could have meant. I look back at him and for what feels like the first time in about a hundred years, I smile. 'You're right. I don't.'

It's the last day of our week here, and there's something I need to do.

'I'm going to see Autumn,' I say to Mum and Dad. They're sitting cuddled up together on the sofa, looking at a parenting magazine. Craig's fixing a miniature digger on the floor. I stop to look at them all. Mum's face is so content. Will it stay that way? Will *they* stay that way – in love, relaxed, *together*?

'Send our love to them all,' Mum says, looking up from her happy haze. I smile back at her, and as I do, it's almost as if I can see the future in her eyes. And I realise that there's no reason for anything to go wrong, now that Mikey's OK. No reason for Mum to drive herself crazy worrying about losing a child. Mum and Dad will be just fine – I'll make sure of it!

I go over and kiss them both. 'Will do,' I say. And then I head over to Autumn's apartment – in the normal lift. There's no way I'm going in that other one ever again!

There's music coming from inside, and a smell of incense wafting out. I smile at the signs of Leonard family normality as I knock.

Autumn's mum opens the door. 'Hi, Jenni,' she smiles. 'Come on in.'

Autumn's on the sofa sitting next to Mikey. They're watching a cartoon together. Mikey's got a bandage round his head and a very grumpy look on his face.

'How you doing Mikey?' I ask, sitting down to join them.

He grunts something unintelligible in reply.

'He's so miserable,' Autumn says. 'His head's too sore for him to play on his games, or run round doing anything interesting.'

'Did they say how long till he'll feel OK?'

'Couple of weeks at most, they reckon. Then he'll be totally normal again. Well, as normal as Mikey could ever be!' Autumn smiles at me. 'One of the nurses said you were a heroine,' she says. 'I told her you're my best friend and she said I'm the luckiest girl in Britain to have such a great best friend.'

Her words are like the sunshine, warming me up inside.

'I told her she was wrong, though,' Autumn says, a mischievous glint in her eyes.

My warm feeling evaporates on the spot. 'Oh.'

Then Autumn smiles so brightly the room lifts another notch in colour and light. 'I told her I'm the luckiest girl in the WORLD!'

I grin back at her. 'So am I,' I say. And for the first time, I realise what being best friends means. It's not about thinking that she's the most amazing person ever, and I'm the luckiest person alive because she's my best friend. *No one*'s the most amazing person ever. We're all just who we are. I still think she's brilliant. But I deserve her because – you know what? – I'm not bad, either.

'Best friends for ever,' Autumn says.

'Absolutely. Nothing will ever get in the way of that,' I say, meaning it more than she will ever know. 'Nothing.'

Autumn flops back into the sofa. 'So, what do you feel like doing today?' she asks casually.

For a moment, I hesitate. When was the last time Autumn asked *me* what we were doing? I don't think I can remember a time. Then I smile as I realise how many things I've changed.

I get up. 'Follow me,' I say.

Autumn jumps up and stands in line behind me. 'Ooh, follow the leader. Fab!' I start walking across the room and Autumn follows behind me, bouncing up and down in a funny walk that makes even Mikey laugh as he watches us.

I lead Autumn out of the room, out of the apartment and out into the beautiful day. Across the road, Mr Barraclough is walking towards the reception block. He gives us a quick wave and goes inside.

That's when I realise there's still something I've got to do.

'I just need to nip in there,' I say as we pass the reception block. 'I'll be back in a minute.'

I've got to try it. I owe it to her, and to myself.

He's just inside the hallway.

'Mr Barraclough!'

He turns and smiles. 'Jenni, hi. How's Mikey doing?'

'He's fine,' I say.

'Just a bandaged up head, eh?' Mr Barraclough says.

'I guess it could have been worse.'

'Yes, it could,' I agree. 'A lot worse.' I fumble to reach into my pocket. 'I've got something for you.'

'For me?' Mr Barraclough watches as I pull something out.

'It's a letter,' I say. 'But you've got to do exactly what I say.'

He stifles a laugh. 'Exactly what you say?'

'Please,' I insist. 'It's important.'

I hand him the letter. 'Read it now,' I say. 'On your own. And then you have to go up to the first floor, apartment 110 and take the letter with you.'

Mr Barraclough's staring at the folded pages. 'Who's this from?' he asks, suddenly serious. 'Where did you get it?'

'It'll all be explained if you do what I say. Apartment 110, OK?'

'Right, right,' he says, wandering away, still staring at the letter.

'Mr Barraclough,' I call after him.

He stops, turns.

'I've not told you the most important thing.'

'And that is?'

'Use the lift,' I say carefully.

'Yes, yes, if you insist.' He turns away again.

'Listen!' I call after him. He stops again. 'The *old* one,' I say. 'The one that doesn't work. Use that one.' He stares hard at me then, as though he's looking for something more in my words. 'Very well,' he says eventually, holding my eyes. 'I will.'

We've been sitting talking and watching the weir rush by for the last hour. Autumn hasn't suggested we try to cross it. Even *she* wouldn't do it when it's this full. She hasn't suggested we climb any trees or leap any fences, either. But even if she did, I wouldn't mind. The last few days have made me realise that I can do a lot more than I'd thought.

Autumn suddenly jumps to her feet. 'Come on, let's move on.'

Two people are coming towards us as we head up the path. As they get closer, I see it's Christine and Sally. 'Hi,' they say, smiling at Autumn and blanking me, as usual.

'Come on, Autumn,' I say, heading the opposite way.

'Oooohh, don't answer us then!' Christine snorts, sticking her nose in the air.

'What was that for?' Autumn asks.

I shake my head. 'I don't know. Sorry. I just don't think much of them.'

'Bit snooty just then, wasn't she?' Autumn says, watching as they walk off, giggling together.

'Well, that's what people are like when they're not real friends.'

We're passing the front doors to Autumn's block when there's a clunking noise from inside. Through the glass door, we see the old lift being opened.

'I thought that one didn't work,' Autumn says.

'Must have fixed it,' I reply casually as two people emerge from the lift. Mr Barraclough – and Mrs Smith! They're smiling at each other, lost in a world of their own.

Mr Barraclough stops to hold the door for her and they come outside. His eyes are radiant, his smile seems to light the space around them. I've never seen him smile like that. And I've never seen two people who look so much as though they belong together.

They don't notice Autumn and me. I guess Mrs Smith wouldn't remember me anyway. Maybe in her world, it didn't even happen.

But as they amble slowly up the path, Mrs Smith looks back over her shoulder. Catching my eye, she smiles at me so broadly I can't help grinning back at her. Her face is a mix of happiness, confusion and gratitude. *She does remember me!* Then, when no one's looking, she mouths, *Was this you?*

That's when I realise – of course! Mr Barraclough only went forward a year. She hadn't even written her letter then! I nod, and give her a sneaky thumbs up in reply. I did it! I really did it. I changed *everything*!

Mrs Smith mouths, *Thank you* and smiles. Then she turns back to Mr Barraclough. He takes her hand in his as they walk away.

Autumn nudges me and points to their locked hands. 'Who's that, then?'

'Mr Barraclough's wife, perhaps?' I say, smiling.

She gasps. 'Wife? I didn't know he was married.'

'I'm pretty sure he isn't,' I say. 'But I've got the feeling he might be soon.'

We carry on up the path. As we walk along, the questions slip into my mind. Will I ever tell Autumn the truth about what happened? Would she believe me if I did? Would it make her angry like last time or would it be the best secret in the world to share?

'Come on, let's go to our place,' Autumn says, and I remember the last time we went there. When was it? Yesterday? Last week? *Next year?*

And then I can't help laughing to myself as I realise that none of the questions matter now. The past is over and done with, and the future will look after itself. The present is all we've got – and, right now, it's all I want.

Autumn turns to look at me. 'What're you laughing at?' she asks.

'Everything!' I say, looking around me at all the things that are back to normal. 'The fact that the car parking spaces aren't marked out, and the ivy isn't too bushy – and your dad owns a bright red Porsche.'

'Weirdo!' Autumn rolls her eyes and nudges me in the ribs. 'How on earth did I get lumbered with you as my best friend?' she asks with a laugh.

I punch her on the arm. 'I dunno,' I say, quickening my step as we cross over the bridge and head for our place by the river. 'I guess you could call it good timing.'

Acknowledgements

I would like to thank…

My family, for all sorts of reading and listening and pointing out of things during the process of writing this book – even though they've probably forgotten that they did most of it, as I did start writing it a long time ago!

Fiona Kennedy, for deciding that actually the book really was worth publishing after all;

Amber Caravéo, for helping me to make it the best it could possibly be;

Catherine Clarke, for still and always being the best, nicest, most supportive and generally fabbest agent ever;

Jonathan Engler and Meliora Thomas, for helping me with my medical facts. (If I've got any wrong, it will be because I didn't listen properly. They know their stuff!);

Laura Tonge, for doing, saying and being all the right things at all the right times;

And the usual writer buddies, for the usual support, encouragement, feedback and general sharing of the agonies and ecstasies of this writing lark.

Also by Liz Kessler

Emily Windsnap has lived on a boat her whole
life – yet her mother seems oddly anxious to keep
her away from the water. When she is finally allowed
to have swimming lessons, Emily makes a
startling discovery – she has a tail!

A breathlessly exciting magical adventure story.

Why not collect all the Emily Windsnap books?

The Tail of Emily Windsnap
Emily Windsnap and the Monster from the Deep
Emily Windsnap and the Castle in the Mist
Emily Windsnap and the Siren's Secret
Emily Windsnap's Friendship Book

Imagine if a fairy granted you three wishes . . .
This is what happens to Philippa Fisher when
Daisy, the new girl at school, announces that
she has come to be her fairy godsister.

A story that sparkles with magic and is all
about friendship, luck and how we decide
what we really, really want.

Don't miss all three Philippa Fisher adventures . . .

Philippa Fisher's Fairy Godsister
Philippa Fisher and the Dream Maker's Daughter
Philippa Fisher and the Stone Fairy's Promise